D0325854

THAW

THAW

Monica M. Roe

FRONT STREET
Asheville, North Carolina

In memory of Betsy Hartigan

ACKNOWLEDGMENTS

Sincere thanks are owed to so many of the
wonderful people that I'm blessed to know and love.

To Karen, Katie, Tracey, C. Kelly, Tory, and Matt for continuous friendship,
love, and support. To Tessa and Z, for literary and technical help that I
wouldn't want to have gotten anywhere else. To Mom and Dad, for instilling
in me a love of books and for exposing me to both sides of the world. To my
family and friends in health care—Ellen, Tracey (again), Amery, and Kevin—
who read and corrected early drafts for clinical accuracy.

Special thanks to Nancy Butts, who made this book become a reality, Stephen
Roos, who helped me through the earliest parts, and the English teachers of
Whitney Point Central School, especially Nancy Hanover and Ron Orzel.

Copyright © 2008 by Monica M. Roe
All rights reserved
Printed in the United States of America
Designed by Helen Robinson
First edition

Library of Congress Cataloging-in-Publication Data is available

ISBN-13: 978-1-59078-496-9 (hardcover : alk. paper)

FRONT STREET
An Imprint of Boyds Mills Press, Inc.
815 Church Street
Honesdale, Pennsylvania 18431

THAW

FLORIDA

March 15, after midnight

The back doors of the ambulance scrape open, letting in the hum of crickets and a rush of warm, humid air. Quite a change from the New York snow we left behind this morning. Sticky, but it feels good after three hours of bouncing along the shitty roads from the Tampa airport in this refrigerated tomb.

At least it feels like three hours. I have no way of knowing. Even if I were wearing a watch, I couldn't move my head or my arm to bring the two closer together. The tips of a few fingers have started to flutter when I try and move them, but that's about all I've got.

"Is that the kid?" The voice comes from outside. I can't see who it belongs to.

"Who else would it be?" This from the Cro-Magnon in the Emergency Medical Services jacket who's sitting in here with me. Him I *have* been able to see since the pothole that bounced my head sideways. This forced me to spend the remainder of the trip staring at the pile of Dorito crumbs accumulating on his crotch as he crunched his way through a full-size bag.

Bigfoot lumbers to his feet, showering the floor with orange bits, and jumps out the back. There's a count of three and the gurney's yanked into the wet night air, sliding me with it like a corpse in a morgue drawer, my head flopping back so I'm staring up again. Directly into a round and extremely bright light attached to the side of the brick building we've parked next to. My eyes immediately start to water from the glare and I squeeze them shut, but wetness still slides from under my eyelids down toward my ears. Wheels rattle, and I'm moving up a ramp, every bump jarring through my aching body. Sounds like an automatic door whooshing open in front of us, then a blast of cold, sterile air.

Pain explodes in my left hand. I yell, eyes flying open to stare at a white-tiled ceiling and the nose hairs of the brilliant individual who just crunched my hand between the gurney and the door frame.

"What? What is it?" His dumb face blinks down at me, momentarily mystified, before seeing the problem. "Oh. Bet that hurt. You should really keep your hands on the bed."

I can't move my hands, you moronic circus chimp. That's what I want to scream up at him. But I still can't talk much over a whisper—that yell was really more of a croak—and it takes me forever to say anything.

If I've learned one thing in the three weeks I've been like this, it's that people don't bother listening to you when they have to wait around for the words to come. So I just close my eyes again, which are now watering from pain instead of light. It isn't worth the effort, anyway.

We're inside and rolling again. One of the wheels on this thing is bad—it keeps rattling around and pulling to the side. Good thing I'm strapped down, or Bigfoot and the Hand-Smashing Wonder would probably dump me onto the floor.

The rattling stops, and I hear the idiot twins talking to

someone, pens scratching on clipboards like they're signing for a FedEx delivery. Why, yes, we did order one pile of eighteen-year-old human male tissue—the blond, blue-eyed variety.

"Dane Rafferty, right?" This voice is female.

Bigfoot grunts an affirmative.

"Parents didn't come with him?"

"Nope. Still back in New York. Life goes on, right?"

"What's this?"

I open my eyes for a second. Along with the glare from the overhead track lights, I see a dark-haired nurse holding up my squashed hand, examining an oozing red scrape.

"Got knocked in the door. He was hanging it off the gurney."

The nurse snorts, apparently unimpressed with this explanation. "I think we can take it from here," she says, her voice clearly dismissing them.

The cerebral derelicts finish up and fade out, their footsteps echoing down the hall. She leans directly over me.

"Dane?"

I don't want to stare into that stupid light again, but it's been days since someone's actually talked *to* me, rather than over or about me. I crack my eyelids and squint up at her. I think the nametag dangling above my chest says Sara.

"Can you talk?"

I swallow and try to wet cracked lips with a dry tongue. The breathing tube just came out of my throat this morning, and everything's still sore as hell.

"Some." The word comes out crackled and peeling like sloughed birch bark. The voice, just like everything else, doesn't even belong to me anymore.

Sara nods. "Probably still hurts a lot. That'll go away in a day or two." She looks young, with pieces of dark hair falling out of her ponytail and around her face. Just like Elise's.

"You've got to be exhausted. Let's get you settled so you can get some rest." She dips out of view, then returns with reinforcements.

I hate being moved from one bed to another, rolled back and forth as they try to jam a sheet under me, and the stupid short gown rides up to expose the piss tube that snakes between my legs. As they grab the corners of the sheet and pull, I close my eyes and hope someone will remember to hold my head so it won't bounce off a bedrail or get caught under a stray elbow. Both have happened before.

This time, though, all goes well. I hear two thuds that sound like my gym bag and backpack being dropped, then everyone clears out except Sara, who raises up the head of the bed a little so I'm looking at her instead of the ceiling. A stinging wetness rubs across my hand.

"Sorry!" Sara says. "I know that hurts. I'll be quick, okay?" I can almost pretend her bent head is Elise's, how she used to lean over to kiss my fingertips when she thought I was sleeping.

Sara finishes taping some gauze over my hand and stands up. "I have to go now," she says. "I'll check back on you soon." She starts to turn away, stops. "You need anything before I leave?"

My mouth's sticky-dry and my neck's twisted funny and my whole body feels like it's been kicked. But I don't tell her about any of that. It takes a while for me to string enough words together to say what I want, but she finally gets the point and retrieves my backpack from the floor. "In here?"

"Side ... part ..."

She unzips the small pocket and pulls out the carved wooden loon. "Isn't that pretty," she says, perching it on her palm. "You want it on your nightstand?"

"No ..." I'm too tired to say anything more, but Sara sees me flexing the tips of my fingers and understands. She curls my hand around the little white-speckled black bird. But then she strokes my arm. I guess she's trying to be comforting or something, but it actually makes my skin itch like hell.

"I'll come back soon and unpack your things, okay?" She can take that look off her face any time now. I don't need any goddamned pity from her or anyone else.

She leaves the door open when she leaves, letting a narrow wedge of light leak in from the hallway. I stare at the shadowy ceiling. The loon feels warm and smooth against my palm. I'm an idiot for bringing the worthless thing with me in the first place. As much as I wanted to hold it a second ago, suddenly its very presence pisses me off. But it's not like I can even open my hand to let go of it, much less break it against the wall.

Elise brought it two weeks ago. Right before the bitch kissed me, tears dropping off her cheeks for proper dramatic effect, then walked out.

March 18, 7:05 a.m.

"Rise and shine, sweet thing!"

The window shades fly up with a snap, flooding my room and my eyes with sunlight.

I squeeze my eyes shut. "Beat it, Godzilla." I've been here three days now, and Letitia, the morning nurse, still can't get it through her head that she doesn't need to barge in every morning like she's storming the castle.

She looms over my bed. Today's nurse suit is dark purple and makes her resemble an obese eggplant. I tell her so.

"Now, you don't mean that, sugar," she says, pinching my cheek. How I'd love to be able to grab her fingers and break them. Or at least bite her.

"Want to bet?" At least my voice has been getting better, even if the rest of me hasn't started yet.

Letitia laughs. "I never bet this early in the morning, honey." She disappears into the bathroom. Over the sound of running water, she shouts, "Now, put on a happy face, not that I've ever seen one on you, and let's get your pretty self ready for the day."

I absolutely cannot stand her.

I'm not about to get into the gruesome details of having one's

entire morning hygiene routine performed by a female cross
between George Foreman and Jabba the Hutt. Suffice it to say
that some stuff goes into me, some comes out, and Letitia's version of a sponge bath nearly drowns me.

"Ain't you gonna let me shave that scraggly face of yours? You
look like my grandmama's pincushion."

"You touch my face with that thing and I'll spit on you."

"How 'bout I change up that music for you? You had the same
stuff playin' two days now."

"Leave it!" It feels spectacular to finally be able to yell at
someone.

Letitia eventually gets out and I'm right back where I started
before she barged in, albeit somewhat cleaner and substantially
more annoyed. It's a mystery to me exactly why I should be
woken up and tortured at the crack of dawn when I'm just going
to spend the rest of the day flat on my back.

It's also hard to believe that less than a month ago, it was virtually impossible to catch me in bed after six in the morning. Like
everything else, that reality belongs to my life pre-GBS.

Guillain-Barré Syndrome. Stupid name for a disease. It's
always cracked me up how arrogant scientists are, ever anxious to
slap their names onto absolutely anything, just to prove they were
the first to notice it. Doesn't matter if it's the cure for AIDS or a
new species of sea slug.

Or a crazy disease that turns your body's own immune system
against you, your cells eating their way up your nerves like a
deranged game of Pac-Man until you're completely paralyzed,
can't talk, can't even breathe without some machine doing the
job for you.

Not that anyone's bothered to explain things to me, but from what I've overheard, the whole process actually started a few weeks before I even knew anything was wrong. By the time I did, it was almost too late.

Fortunately, almost doesn't count for much, whether it's winning or dying. And since I didn't die, now I'm playing the waiting game. That's the weirdest thing about Guillain-Barré. After a few weeks, the whole thing starts reversing itself. It's already happening for me—a week ago, I couldn't talk or breathe on my own, and now I've got both back. The rest of my muscles will be next. Cool process, if you look at it scientifically.

Don't get me wrong. It was scary as hell at first, and I've put up with a lot of shit during the whole mess, but at least I know this isn't permanent. I heard some doctor tell my parents that about 75 percent of people who get GBS make a full recovery. Those odds shouldn't be too hard to beat.

So now I wait.

What's annoying is where I'm waiting. I've been sent halfway across the country to a rehab hospital in desolate central Florida, theoretically because it's the best.

But also, just possibly, so my parents won't be inconvenienced. No doubt they'd prefer to get me back fully fixed and able to fulfill my role in the family symbiosis. Like my mom said when they shipped me off from the hospital back in upstate, "We'll see you as soon as you're up and running, dear."

She must have gotten caught up in the drama of the moment, because she actually kissed me, which was sort of amusing.

But for whatever reasons, here I am. Waiting. And if I can keep these freaking hospital people from driving me insane, I'll be okay.

March 21, 10:00 a.m.

"Dane Rafferty?"

My eyes are closed, but I know someone's lurking in my doorway. I contemplate my inner eyelids, hoping this one will be smart enough to get the point.

No such luck. The sound of a butt hitting a chair tells me someone's making herself way too comfortable. I wait awhile, but she doesn't show a tendency toward getting the hell out of my room. Damn.

After at least five minutes, curiosity finally gets the better of me. I open my eyes directly into a pair of intensely blue ones.

"Oh, good. I was starting to think you were dead." The eyes and the voice belong to this chick who looks about twenty-seven or so. Her hair's red and straight, held back with a silver-colored metal band, and she's got just a few freckles, putting her somewhere between a pixie and a dominatrix.

"Who the hell are you?"

"Nice to meet you, too." Her voice is smooth, slightly mocking. "I'm Anya Gray—your physical therapist. But we can pass on the rest of the formalities for now. We'll get to know each other quite well over the next few months." She gets out of my face and starts looking me over like a butcher trying to decide which way to carve up the cow.

"I'll pass on everything, thanks." Some therapist used to come into my hospital room back in New York. As far as I could tell, all he ever did was bend my body parts a bit. Looked like a lot of nothing, plus it hurt.

Anya either doesn't get the hint or doesn't take it. "You're not feeling up to it today?"

"Or any day. Turn the iPod on when you leave, would you?" I use a newfound ability to turn my head (that happened yesterday) and look out the window. The one good thing about this place so far is that my room has an incredible view of a huge pond, which gives me all kinds of great stuff to watch. I saw an alligator nosing around the reeds yesterday, and I'm hoping he'll be back.

Anya walks around the bed and snaps the window shade down.

"Hey!"

"Maybe they don't teach manners up north, but it's generally considered polite to not ignore someone when they're talking to you." She sits backward on another chair and folds her arms across the back. "Now let's start over. I'm Anya."

Whatever this little game is, I'm sure as hell not playing. "It's generally considered polite to not barge into someone's room and bore them when you aren't wanted. Therefore, you can leave." I turn my head the other way, so I'm looking toward the hallway.

I hear Anya suck in her breath. She's pissed.

Good.

I wait.

"You know," she says, her voice wound tight like she's trying to keep it reined in, "I'm not here for a social visit. Have you noticed that your body doesn't exactly work at the moment? Just how do you propose to get better if you don't plan on doing rehab?"

"Save it, babe." Like I've said before, I've kept my ears open, and I know how this disease goes. "All I'm doing now is waiting for stuff to come back. That's going to happen whether or not you bring your ass in here and move me around a little, so why don't you just save us both the trouble?" Truthfully, she's hot enough that it wouldn't be such a hardship to have her hands on me a couple times a day. But I don't like her attitude, so she can forget it.

Anya snorts. "Oh, you think everything's just going to come back on its own? Just like magic, all your muscles are going to wake up and be good as new, and you'll be back on skis with no problem?"

That's exactly what has to happen. I won't accept any other option.

But she keeps talking. "If that were true, why would I have a job?"

I don't need this.

"Damned if I know," I tell her. "I'm betting they hired you more for your decorative qualities than for your intelligence. Or personality." I don't know how she knows I'm a skier, but this conversation lost my interest a long time ago. "But as far as this room goes, you don't have much of a useful function. Now this has been lovely, truly, but you're boring me. So why don't you turn your ass around and find the door. At least that'll give me something to look at." I smile angelically at her.

I know I've scored a hit, because the PT Princess looks like she's about to turn into ice. "Fine," she says, her voice rigid. "Then let's stop wasting our time, shall we?" She stands, shoves the chair into the corner hard enough to dent the wall, and, trying to look like she meant to all along, *backs* slowly out the door.

God, that's hilarious. Thinks she's quite clever, backing away so I don't check out her assets. I'm amused by a long-ago fact from my mother, the literature professor, who always believed that poetry and literary history made excellent bedtime stories. Backing out of a room was what underlings did in the Elizabethan courts, since they weren't worthy to turn their backs on royalty.

How appropriate.

Anya stops briefly at the door. "I'll be interested to know how your ankles feel in a few days. Maybe you'll find that amusing, too." Then she's gone.

Sometimes it's just too damned easy to mess with people.

Having disposed of her, I'm once again free to watch the pond, which is an ever-changing performance. At the moment, three good-size turtles are stacked up on a drifting log, legs stretched out like miniature supermen as they bask in the sun. They're toward the middle of the pond, so I can't tell what kind they are. Watching them, I think of my own turtle back home. I hope Eric's doing a decent job of taking care of him. The last thing I need is a case of shell rot or a respiratory infection to deal with when I get back.

I laugh then, thinking that these Florida turtles have a lot more to worry about than shell rot. If that alligator decides to put in another appearance, you can bet he'll gladly help himself to a few shelled chew toys.

An intense pain, tingling and electric, suddenly needles into my right calf, making me flinch. My breathing tries to speed up on me, but I catch it, forcing it back into the right rhythm. I close my teeth onto the insides of my cheeks and focus.

Never lose control.

God, I hate when this happens. I know it means my nerves are starting to work again, but I wish they could be a little more organized about it because these random jolts hurt like hell.

I've gotten good at it, though. It's just like any other problem— you deal with it the smartest way possible. So what if my body won't let me deal with the pain right now? I use my mind instead. If I didn't know how to do that, I would have gone over the edge way before now.

It's all about intelligence and self-control and the most logical course of action. Too bad Cabot Forrester never understood that. If he had, he probably could have saved himself—not to mention the rest of our team—a whole lot of trouble.

Thinking about Cabot makes me think about Nordic skiing, and suddenly my mind's taken me away from this bed in this room in this hospital in the middle of this weird-warm Florida winter. I'm back in northern New York, my natural habitat, on the day of my last perfect run before this whole mess started—when I was untouchable, a deity on skis, and Elise was still there with me.

UPSTATE NEW YORK

February 10, 2:35 p.m.

We're three miles into the run, and this prick from Northwood thinks he owns the race. He's starting to get sloppy, slowing up on his turns, breaking stride every now and then. Idiot hasn't even noticed me pacing him, hanging back about fifty yards and making good use of the trail he's so kindly cutting through the snow for me. That's just fine. Let him get cocky; let him forget there's anyone behind him.

Let me play with him a bit.

That'll just make it sweeter when I dust his ass.

The powder's not the best today—last night's sleet frosted it with a tough crust, just weak enough to let my edges break through, too strong to let them sink all the way to the frozen dirt beneath. The snow squeaks as my skis slash through it, little balls of ice beading and skittering away behind me in a shimmering wake. Conditions are just slippery enough to be a little bit dangerous. Just the way I like it. When the snow makes you pay attention, makes you think—that's when you can really whip out what you can do.

I've got my rhythm perfectly, body tucked low in a crouch, head ducked into the wind, the familiar faint burn in my quads

and calves as my legs power down through the snow, shoving my
skis forward.

I'm feeling strong, really strong. My wind's good, and it feels like I can keep this up forever, like I can just keep skiing until I reach the edge of the world and drop off. It's good to be back on my game after last week. Guess I've finally gotten over that flu-thing that knocked me on my ass for a few days. Funny, since I almost never get sick.

The wind kicks up as I make for the top of the next hill, whirling little bits of snow against my goggles, prickling the exposed part of my face like tiny darts. Ahead of me, the Northwood punk's blue spandex fades in and out of the white whirl. I'll let him think he's in the clear for now. Enjoy it while it lasts.

I crest the hill, catch air briefly, and pound down onto terra firma in a shower of powder. I plummet down the rise into a thick stand of hardwoods and evergreens, ducking overhanging limbs as I descend. This time of year it's harder to tell the deciduous trees apart—especially without my Audubon guide and especially when the scenery is whipping past at warp speed—but the sugar maples are immediately visible with their gray brown, scaly bark, along with the metal sap buckets clustered four feet up their trunks. This part of the course winds through a stretch of privately owned woods, and the owners do some small-scale sugaring each year. I used to help out with sap collection at our neighbors' when I was a kid, and I always thought it tasted even better before it was boiled down into syrup. I used to get busted for sticking my hands into the sap pails to snag a taste.

Come to think of it, I'm a bit thirsty now.

Should I waste the time? I check out Northwood—still

enjoying himself fifty yards up. Behind me, the coast is still clear—the next pack shouldn't be along for at least another minute. There're only two of us who are really in this race, anyway.

Why not? Hell—at least it'll give me a bit of a challenge, playing catch-up. I throw myself into a stop, tossing out a sheet of snow and grinding to a halt in front of a huge maple that's a hundred years old, easy. The trunk is so wide I could reach both arms around it with no hope of my fingers meeting on the far side. Eight pails are laddered around its scarred trunk. Skewering my poles into a nearby snowbank, I reach for the closest pail, lifting it free from the metal spout hammered into the tree. Even through my gloves, I can feel the bite of the frozen metal, cold like fire. I slide the lid back and lift the pail to my mouth, careful not to freeze my tongue to the side. Sap rushes down my throat like quicksilver ice, so cold I can barely taste the subtle sweetness.

It's interesting how everything seems to taste better when you're outside. It's like all the extras, all the superfluous shit people pile on to complicate their lives, have to be left behind before things can be fully enjoyed the way they were intended. Out here, the icy sap straight from the pail is way more satisfying than the designer bottled water I'll get back in the locker room after the race.

After a few mouth-numbing gulps, I replace the bucket on the tree and retrieve my ski poles, stopping briefly to examine a tiny set of tracks crossing the snowbank beside them. They look like they belong to some sort of rodent, but I'm not positive. I make a mental note to look them up when I get home tonight, then check my watch—I've been stopped about forty seconds. From the trail behind me comes the faint swish of skis on snow as the first cluster of racers nears the top of the hill. They'll be coming down any second now. Ahead of me, Northwood has disappeared over the horizon, two parallel tracks and the scattered semicircles punched into the snow from his poles the only evidence of his passing.

I reposition my goggles and swing onto the trail.

Time to get it done.

He's gained enough ground on me that I don't have time to consider form or finesse as I narrow the gap. But that's okay. For now, I abandon the stylistic stuff and funnel everything I've got into a raw outpouring of speed. My mind clears itself of everything else around me, then narrows in until its entire focus melds with the trail and my body hurtling forward. My breathing's in sync with my skis and I'm part of the trail.

Then I simply run Northwood down. He doesn't even know I'm coming until he's spitting out the powder from my wake. The finish tape breaks across my chest a full three seconds ahead of him, and I've won.

Again.

"Nice run." Northwood's clenched-teeth congratulations don't exactly sound sincere. He sounds as if he would happily bayonet me with his ski pole were it not for the large number of witnesses present.

I act like I don't see his outstretched glove, which—let's face it—he's only got stuck out there for PR purposes, anyway. "I know." I take leave of Mr. Second Best *sans* closing remarks and cruise over to the sidelines to lose my skis and watch the rest of the team come in.

From the spectator area, Elise peels out of the crowd and runs over, her usually pale face flushed pink from the cold. She jumps and throws her arms around me, almost knocking me down.

"Hey, you did it again!" Her lips brush the air beside my face, but I manage to turn my head fast enough so they don't make contact, though I do get a brief mouthful of her hair.

"Come on, Elise. You know I hate that shit." I duck away from her arm, spitting out a wavy brown strand, and finish taking off my goggles.

"Oh, right. I forgot there's a rule about kissing your boyfriend only at appointed times." Elise backs off a step, fishes a Gatorade from her backpack, then reaches into the pocket of her black fleece and pulls out a PowerBar. "Here. I thought you could use these." She tosses them at me, maybe just a little harder than necessary.

We've been together over a year now, and she never seems to remember that I can't stand that public display, look-at-me-I-own-kissing-rights-to-Dane-Rafferty crap. And then she gets snippy when I have to remind her.

But she did bring me food, and I'm starving. "Perfect." I down the Gatorade in one go, then tear the wrapper off the energy bar.

Elise scans the crowd of spectators, shading her eyes against the white glare of the snow. "Your family was here a second ago. I thought they were right behind me."

"Were they?" I'm only half listening to her. My attention's focused on the finish line, where the first group of skiers is sliding home in clumps of two and three, strung out like a bunch of multicolored amoebas. The amoebas look to be more red than blue, green, or black at the moment. Good—we're ahead. Jeff and Ash are the first from our team to come in after me. Justin and

McNeal aren't far behind them. I can't see Forrester yet, which is bad news. He needs to get his times down. He messed up his Achilles tendon earlier in the season, and it's been giving him trouble ever since. Or rather, it's been giving the whole team trouble because he's been slow as hell.

I had a talk with him about it before the race, so hopefully he'll get it together and come through for us today. I recheck the group of finishers on the off chance that I missed him the first time around. Nope. He's still dicking around somewhere out on the run. Wonderful.

Coach walks over, sunlight reflecting off his Oakleys. "Another nice one, Rafferty—well done." He sticks his clipboard under his arm and shakes my hand. "You keep this up, and you'll pretty much be untouchable by the end of the season." He smiles at Elise. "Of course, having this young lady waiting for you at the finish line must be a little added incentive, huh?"

Like I need any incentive to make me perform better. "How was my time?"

"Very satisfactory." It isn't Coach who answers. I spin around.

"Hey, Dad. Eric. Didn't see you when I came in."

My father has his stopwatch in his hand. He tosses it to me so I can see the time it registers. "Not your best time, son, but still good. Definitely good."

He would be less than thrilled if he knew I'd tacked over half a minute onto my time voluntarily. But what I do in the privacy of the woods is my own affair. Besides, I get a bit of a kick out of how closely he pays attention to each individual race.

Just like everyone else, he actually thinks I have to give it my all to win every time.

26

"You feeling okay?" my fourteen-year-old brother, Eric, asks. He's the only one who knows how shitty I felt all last week, and that's only because he caught me heaving once when he got up to use our bathroom in the middle of the night.

"No problem," I tell him, giving him a look so he doesn't make a big deal out of it.

Coach breaks in. "Well, I'd better go see how everyone else is doing. I'm a little worried about Cabot and that ankle of his." He slaps me on the back and jogs off toward the finish area.

I swap my ski boots for my hiking boots, then gather my gear and pack it in my ski bag. "Look, guys, I'll probably be here awhile. Why don't you go on home?"

Dad checks his watch. "Don't be too late—your mother's actually cooking tonight."

"Okay." They head off toward the parking lot, leaving Elise and me by ourselves.

"We still on for tomorrow?" I ask her. We're planning to go snowshoe Azure. The forecast is calling for a totally clear day, and we're hoping to catch a good sunrise from the top of the mountain.

She picks a loose thread from her fleece and nods. "Definitely. Don't forget, I have to be back for my CPR re-cert by three." Elise guides rafting trips every summer, so she always has to stay current with her CPR and first aid.

"Okay." I swing my bag over my shoulder. "Then we should get going early. Pick you up around five?"

"Sure. I'll bring lunch, since you're driving."

"Deal. Guess I'll see you then."

"I can wait for you now if you're not busy," Elise says.

I'm not really, but I'd rather just hang by myself for a bit—I usually do after a race. "No, that's okay—just go ahead. I'll see you tomorrow." Before she can say anything else or try to kiss me again, I give her a quick wave and head over to where the rest of the team has gathered.

I've gotten so used to coming in first that it's no big thing anymore. Everyone else seems to get more excited about it than I do. As busy as he is, Dad always comes to my meets, and he keeps closer track of my times than I do. Coach is dead certain I'll get offered a scholarship to ski for Dartmouth or St. Lawrence or Colby—one of those New England WASP schools that prize winter sports and the wealthy white kids who can afford both the equipment and the requisite years of lessons. I don't bother myself with that too much, and I don't care about nit-picking my times, either. I don't need a sports scholarship to go to college, anyway. I know I'm the best, and as long as that's the case, I'm fine with it. The only time I have to start splitting hairs and nickel-and-diming the minutes and seconds is when one of the other guys starts slipping up and I have to make up the difference, which is annoying as hell.

Which reminds me. I still don't see Cabot Forrester at the finish line.

Jeff hasn't gotten his skis off. He slides over to meet me and punches me on the shoulder with his wet glove. "Way to go, brother. Looks like you pulled down another one, huh?"

"Guess so." I toss my bag onto the snow and pull my sunglasses from my pocket. "How we doing?"

Jeff plays with the tassel of his hat. "Still in first place. Comfortably, too. There was yours, of course. And Ash and I both pulled down our best times of the season!" He grins proudly.

"Good." I scan the finish line again. "Where the hell is Forrester? Is he even in this race?" There's still no sign of him. Jesus.

Jeff's smile disappears. "I'm not sure, Dane. I was hanging next to him for a while at the beginning, and it looked like he was having a rough go of it. I hope he's okay."

"Well, it'd certainly be nice if he finishes sometime this year." It never ceases to amaze me how short the supply of competence in this world is. If I think about it too much, it just depresses me.

And I'm still hungry. "You want to grab something to eat after we finish here?" I ask.

Jeff shakes his head, making his tassel bounce. "Sorry. I'm picking Angie up after this. I'll probably be late as it is."

Like Angelica's really worth being on time for. "I don't know, Jeff—I worry about you, buddy. Are you ever going to get rid of that one?" Angelica's not much of a high-ranker in any area, as far as I'm concerned. I honestly don't know how Jeff's been able to stand being with her for as long as he has. Rumor has it she's been around the block more times than you'd care to count, and I have no idea why that doesn't put up any red flags for Jeff. With all the crazy shit that can go wrong when you start seriously hooking up with someone, you at least want to be sure that anyone you choose is going to be disease-free and have the brains to remember to take her birth control.

That's one of the cool things about Elise. I'm her first, and she's way too smart to let herself get pregnant.

Jeff leans down and frees his feet from his bindings. "Winter's long and cold around these parts, Raff. Sometimes you have to take what's available. We can't all be as lucky as you. Girls like Elise are few and far between, you know?"

"Yeah, she's all right."

All the guys seem to really like Elise. I guess it's not that surprising. She's good-looking without spending a ton of time working at it, and her cosmetic bag's got waterproof matches and a pocketknife in it alongside the very few makeup things she keeps around for weddings and funerals. She's smart, confident, and sexy as hell to a certain kind of guy, which most of my friends have certainly noticed. But there's no worry there. I'm Elise's first long-term thing, and she's totally into me and us and all that garbage. I don't think she even knows that other guys exist, in the non-Platonic realm, that is.

Jeff laughs. "All right? Man, if you're ever crazy enough to let that one go, I'll be more than happy to step in and take up the slack."

"Yeah, you wish."

"Damned right I do."

There's an outbreak of voices behind us, and we turn toward the commotion. Three people are crossing the finish line together. The two on the outside are wearing South Franklin black, and they're hunched over against the extra weight of the person they're supporting between them, an arm looped around each of their shoulders.

It's Cabot.

"Oh, shit." Jeff releases his bindings, drops his poles, and jogs toward them, almost tripping because he's still got his ski boots on.

Forrester doesn't have his skis on—probably ditched them out on the trail somewhere. He's hopping on one foot, his face twisted and sweating, breathing hard in short gasps. The Franklin guys

are practically holding him up, and I can tell they're about ready
to give out, too. They must have brought him in a good ways.

Damn it. Sighing, I start after Jeff.

Jeff reaches them a split second after Coach, and the athletic
trainer's right behind them. They ease Forrester off the Franklins'
shoulders and half-carry him over to a bench. He's biting his lip,
and his eyes are shut tight. The trainer unzips his pant leg and
undoes his boot. She eases it off, and Cabot yells, grabbing Jeff's
hand and squeezing.

It's times like this when I wish that we humans operated on
the same wavelength as the rest of the animal kingdom. Darwin
really had it right. Survival of the fittest—the strong herd members survive and pass on their genes; the weak ones get picked
off. Political correctness and everything aside, isn't that really
the better way to run things? Why can't we just cull out the dead
weight so the rest of us can achieve the way we're meant to?

But no, that wouldn't do. Instead, we had to have Forrester
trying to ski on a blown ankle, then hurting himself more and
screwing things up for those of us who actually can deliver, who
can perform the way we're supposed to. It's frustrating as hell.

All right, enough of this daytime drama. I'm tired and hungry,
and I want to get the hell out of here. I turn and crunch across the
snow, stopping to scoop up my gear bag, then making my way up
the hill toward the entrance to the school locker rooms.

On the bright side, at least those South Franklin guys had to
have pulled their team's score down pretty good.

In spite of Forrester's crap, I think we'll still win this one.

FLORIDA

March 21, 10:23 a.m.

The pain's still knifing through my leg, a slow, glacial burn. I'm sweating, and I think I just bit through my lip.

But I'm still under control.

March 23, 9:07 a.m.

"Give me the damn phone."

"Now, you don't want to go doin' that, honey. Your folks sent you here so you can get fixed up." Ignoring my request, Letitia keeps dragging a comb through my hair, despite my best efforts to shake her dumb hand off my head. "Isaac didn't scare you none, did he? He's harmless—just wanders over here by accident sometimes."

"Of course he didn't scare me, you moron." I'd eat my own IV before admitting it, but it did shake me up a little. Waking up to the sight of a seven-foot stranger standing over you would be disconcerting under any circumstances. But when the stranger has on a purple top hat covered with glued-on beads, feathers, and glitter and is wearing a couple hundred plastic-bead necklaces and bracelets, it gets downright creepy. He was pushing one of those walker things you usually associate with old people, even though he only looked around thirty-five, but even that was painted a violent, sparkly green. He didn't say anything, just stood there sort of giggling to himself, and the overall effect was truly disturbing.

"Well, if you wasn't scared, then where's the problem, sugar?"

Letitia's clearly not interested in a reply because she stuffs a toothbrush into my mouth and starts ramming it into my gums, so all I can do is glare at her and concentrate on not choking on toothpaste spit.

After Isaac was ushered out of my room by some nameless aide who was absolutely terrified of getting busted for losing him in the first place, I finally found out the truth about this place.

It's a loony bin.

I'm not kidding. Supposedly, the place specializes in all sorts of "neurological rehabilitation." What nobody bothered to fill me in on before is that this means "brain injury" for most of the patients here. Since I haven't been out of my room since I got here, I had no idea what a psycho ward I'd landed in until my visit from the giant beaded lunatic. And if he represents what else is wandering around out there, I'm sure as hell not staying.

As soon as Letitia lets up with the toothbrush, I again demand to use the phone, which she really can't refuse, even though she has to prop it against my shoulder and dial the number for me. She stands there as the other end starts ringing, until I hiss at her to get lost.

"Professor Rafferty's office." Dad's voice sounds distracted, but it changes slightly when he hears it's me.

"Dane, how you doing down there? Getting settled in all right?"

"I've been here over a week." I wish I wasn't still so damned slow when I talk.

The phone is silent for a second. "I know. I've been meaning to call, but things got busy up here. I'm in the middle of a grant proposal, and you know what a process that is."

Yeah, I do. It's a process that he usually has very little to do with. Once he decides what kind of research project he wants to tackle, he turns it over to Mom, the literary wonder, who then cranks out stellar proposal outlines and statements of purpose for him that almost never get rejected. That's how their particular interaction has always worked.

When I don't say anything, Dad fills the gap. "Did you call to talk about anything in particular?"

"Yeah. I can't stay here. The place is full of lunatics."

Dad laughs, apparently thinking I'm joking. "Well, I know hospital people aren't the most interesting individuals in the world, but they do have their purpose to serve. Right now, that purpose is to get you back on your feet. How's that going, anyway?" he adds, like he just remembered why they shipped me off in the first place. "You're talking more now, that's good. Anything else coming back?"

I start to tell him about being able to roll my head around, but that doesn't seem sufficiently newsworthy, so instead I try to get back to the reason I called. "I meant the other patients. They all have brain damage or something. They're crazy."

Dad sighs knowingly. "Well, that makes sense. I suppose the neurological injuries there would encompass the whole clinical spectrum from peripheral system interruption like yours to more involved central nervous system damage."

I hate it when he does that, has to show that he knows as much as anyone about anything. He's an ecology professor, for God's sake—anything he knows about the "clinical spectrum" of my "peripheral system interruption" has got to be a few random facts that he grabbed from some pathology textbook so he could impress his colleagues with med-speak about his son's disease.

He continues, "I know it's not easy, but I'm sure you'll be fine, Dane. This is really the best place for you right now."

"Dad, it's not. Why can't I go to Upstate or Fletcher Allen—"

He cuts in before I can finish. "Because you're in the best place for someone in this phase of your condition."

Now he's memorizing condition phases, too?

"Besides, if you were in Syracuse or Burlington, then we'd be running back and forth on the weekends, and that would put a big strain on everyone's schedule—mine, your mother's, even Eric's. I know you wouldn't want that, would you?"

I stare out the window at a huge white bird standing in the shallow water at the edge of the pond. I wonder what it is.

"No." That's what he wants to hear, anyway.

"That's what I thought." Dad's voice is starting to get distracted again, like he's already thinking about something else. "Once you're functional again, we can definitely look into some closer options for the rest of your rehab, okay?"

"Sure. Whatever." Now I'm not listening, concentrating instead on the bird skulking through the water, stabbing at the reeds with a thick, strangely curved bill. I've never seen one quite like it.

"Look, why don't you let me go now. I've got a pile on my desk to get through that you wouldn't believe."

"Okay." I should never have called in the first place.

"Dane? We are anxious for you to get home—all of us." I start to answer, but he hangs up before I have time.

I straighten my neck, sore from death-gripping the phone against my shoulder, and let the receiver slide onto the bed.

March 23, 6:02 p.m.

Something's brewing in the habitat across the hall. Scrub-suited worker bees have been humming in and out all afternoon, juggling machines and sheets and stuff. I wonder what's going to happen.

My world has compressed to two views. Outside I can see the pond, the walkway that circles it, and on the far side, a semicircle of little green cabins where some of the other inhabitants of this circus are housed. I see them being herded back and forth to the main building periodically every day, and it's quite a show. Some of them make old Isaac look downright mundane.

My only other view (unless you count the straight-up ceiling vista, which I don't) is directly to my left side, where I can stare into the hallway. This angle lets me see the nurses' station and the inside of the room across the hall, the one where all the activity's going on. It's been empty since I've been here, and I can only assume that the new action means someone will be moving in soon. That actually wouldn't be bad.

Besides the slight curiosity and anticipation inspired by the events across the hall, today also brought yet another new face. And this one, *finally*, seems like someone I might be able to tolerate.

It had been getting close to dinnertime (though I currently get most of my nutrition via a highly attractive rubber tube pegged directly into my stomach, so dinner was of no consequence to me), and I was watching the pond again. The big white bird was long gone, and I was squinting across the water at something strange that I couldn't quite make out. Long and thin, it rode along above the surface of the pond, occasionally wiggling around in a slithery sort of way. It looked almost like some sort of water snake, but I'd never seen any snake swim with almost half of its body straight out of the water.

Anyway, I'd been following this weird-ass thing around with my eyes for at least half an hour and was no closer to figuring out what it could be, when, with no warning, a head had popped up in my first-floor window. It startled the hell out of me, even though the head wasn't looking my way. It was facing away toward the pond, so all I could see was the top half of a short-sleeved blue shirt, curly hair that was almost black, and a binocular strap. Out on the pond, the mysterious skinny floating thing abruptly disappeared beneath the surface. The nameless person spun around and leaned on the windowsill.

"Did you see that?" he said through the screen. "Now keep watching him." He pulled up the screen, then backed up, got a running start, and vaulted over the windowsill right into my room. I was too surprised by this to tell him to get lost or to say much of anything, for that matter.

Once he was facing me, I could see the guy was in his late twenties, average height. Muscular, but lean rather than bulked up. He jogged over to my bed and unlooped the binoculars from his neck at the same time. He knelt behind me, reaching around and holding the binoculars up in front of my eyes.

"See that clump of weeds to the right? Keep your eyes there." I watched through the binoculars for about half a minute, and the mystery creature popped up. It turned out to be some sort of water bird, only the head and neck visible. It upended its beak, tossing a wriggling fish straight down its gullet.

"Wild, huh?" The guy pulled the binoculars away from my face and came around the bed so he was in front of me.

"Absolutely. What the hell was that?"

"An anhinga." He leaned against the windowsill. "They don't have oil glands to make their feathers buoyant, so they usually swim with their bodies underwater. When I first moved down here, I spent six months thinking all Florida ponds were inhabited by strange, vertically swimming snakes."

I laughed at that, then sobered up, realizing that I could very well have another psycho from this veggie ranch on the loose in my room. I mean, the guy just waltzed up and jumped in my window. There was a certain element of lunacy in that approach.

"What were you doing outside?" I asked carefully, hoping to catch any red flags that screamed ESCAPEE but not sure what I'd do if I did.

He ran a hand through his curly hair, messing it up even more. "Just wrapping things up for the day. I was actually headed home." The guy suddenly smacked his forehead. "Man, I'm an idiot! Forgot to introduce myself, didn't I?"

He walked to the bed, picked up my hand, and shook it. "Joel Costello."

"Dane."

Joel didn't let go of my hand when he was done shaking it.

Instead, he turned it over, bending the fingers back and forth and flexing my wrist. "These are pretty tight, aren't they?"

He was right. Both of my hands had been trying to curl themselves into fists lately. Since I can barely move them myself, I notice it only when someone else moves them.

It hurt. "Hey, knock it off." I wanted to say more than that to this pervert who was getting a kick out of feeling up my arm, but I was also enough of a self-preservationist to not risk pissing off a potentially deranged person—particularly when there were no witnesses in the vicinity. Figured. Whenever I *don't* want Letitia around, I can't get her away from me.

"Sorry." Joel put my hand down. "I just wanted to get a feel for where your motion's at."

"What the hell for?"

Joel smacked himself on the forehead again. "I only half-introduced myself, didn't I?" He grinned at me. "I'm your occupational therapist."

I was skeptical about Joel's claim, but he checked out, and he is my occupational therapist. Apparently, he's supposed to help me get my arms and upper body going again. He did a decent job of explaining how and why he's supposed to do that, so I've decided to give him a chance. Besides, after that stupid phone call with my dad this morning, I'm more anxious than ever to get my ass in gear so I can get the hell out of here.

Joel's a little on the odd side. Besides his window-leaping tendencies, he's the king of the non sequitur—you can never tell what he's going to say next. But that keeps him from being boring. And best of all, the guy's a walking wellspring of information about the weird Florida wildlife I've been watching since I got here, and he's happy to share what he knows. So as long as he's got interesting things to talk about, I don't mind working with him.

And, not least importantly, he's a half-dozen steps up from that ice-bitch Anya they tried to sic on me the other morning. She came in again yesterday, but I just gave her more of the same. Looks as though they finally woke up and decided to give me someone else.

So now I have a tolerable therapist. Time to get to work.

March 23, 9:22 p.m.

The room across the hall is officially inhabited. The arrival process was essentially a repeat of my own, except with the addition of some people who looked more like family members than hospital drones. The place hummed like a beehive for about an hour, but everyone finally cleared out and let me get a look at my new neighbor.

He looks dead.

I'm serious. From what I can see, this guy belongs in a morgue, not a hospital. His mouth is frozen wide open, like he's a Halloween pumpkin. I've been watching him for fifteen minutes now, and I've yet to see him move, although some sort of alarm has gone off once or twice, bringing a nurse hustling into his room each time.

Of course, I couldn't move at all when I got here either (not that my gains since then have been huge). But his body isn't just motionless, it's also seriously messed up. His arms are curled tight against his chest, hands clenched into fists, and his legs are stuck straight out and rigid.

All in all, he looks pretty grotesque, like an exhumed corpse or something. But I keep watching him, maybe to see if he'll move, maybe just because he's there.

One of the guy's eyes falls open a little bit. Because of the way he's facing, it's almost like he's staring at me through that one tiny slit.

Footsteps echo through the empty hallway and two people go back into the dead guy's room. I don't know where they're coming from now, but they were both here earlier for his arrival. The first, a wilted-looking woman in her late thirties, pulls a chair up beside the bed. She strokes the guy's motionless hand, then kisses it. Her lips move silently, as if she's whispering something to him.

The girl with her looks about sixteen. She paces the room like it's two sizes too small, a long braid the color of deerskin whipping behind her. She strums her fingers across the window blinds and they chatter, making the woman jump and say something to her in a voice that's low but sharp. The girl makes a disgusted noise and strides to the door, stopping short for a second when she sees that I've been observing the whole minidrama.

But only for a second. She stalks across the hall and stands in my doorway. I think she's glaring at me, but I'm busy reading the sentence emblazoned in white across her fitted red shirt: *I'll Try Being Nicer If You'll Try Being Smarter.*

Very nice.

I'm not sure if she's waiting for me to say something, which I don't. She looks me over like I'm a Petri dish resident for a few seconds, then makes her point.

"Show's over, asshole." With that eloquent and ladylike speech, she slams my door so hard the frame rattles, leaving me in the dark.

This place is full of pleasant females.

I have a good chuckle about the mystery chick's little temper tantrum. My curiosity about the next room has instantly been piqued, but it looks like I'm done observing. For now, at least. No worries—my door won't stay closed for long once the nurse sees it. Hospital policy.

Until then, I can watch the pond, silver-dusted by an almost-full moon. I turn my head toward the window, but I'm still seeing that unnamed, dead-looking man and his frozen Halloween face. The way his one eye was open reminds me of the party back at Jeff's house, how Angelica looked that night when she and Jeff ended up putting on a show for the whole house, both of them too plastered to know which end was up.

That was also the night that made Elise decide—according to her, of course—that she wanted out.

UPSTATE NEW YORK

February 11, 11:17 p.m.

Before we're halfway up Jeff's front walk, Elise and I can hear the music pulsing from inside. Good thing he lives way out in the sticks. If the Chadbourns had any immediate neighbors, they'd surely be calling to complain by now. Good thing also that Jeff's parents travel a lot and trust their dear son to take care of the family castle in their absence.

Or maybe they just don't give a damn one way or the other. I guess "out of sight, out of mind" is the status quo for most families, isn't it? Especially families with the money and free time to take leaves of absence from one another on a fairly regular basis.

Figures are outlined in the windows behind the living-room curtains, but not too many, and there are only about ten cars parked in the driveway and along the road.

Good. Jeff said he was just inviting the ski team and any female counterparts. A crowd gets much bigger than that, and I don't want anything to do with it. I've learned to never underestimate the stupidity of people in large groups, especially when there's a keg involved.

Elise speaks my thoughts almost exactly. "At least it doesn't look too crowded in there." She pulls the zipper of her red parka up under her chin and shivers as a gust of wind dumps snow onto us from a tree limb overhanging the sidewalk. She brushes powder from her hair with a gloved hand. "How long are we going to stay?"

"We'll see." I'll probably just put in an appearance for an hour or so, but nothing wrong with leaving my options open.

We leave our boots in the entryway and make our way through the living room, nodding hello to the dozen or so people sitting around on the couches and floor, then go on into the kitchen.

"Hey, Raff. We'd about given up on you." Ash is sitting on the butcher-block countertop with his legs dangling down the side, drumming on the lower cabinet with his boots. "Elise," he adds with a nod. She nods back silently.

"You'd never do that, Ash. You know better," I say, leaning on the counter.

He empties his cup and jumps down, then draws two beers from the keg and hands them to me. I set one on the counter, fully planning to abandon it, and pass the other to Elise. She sets hers directly into the sink, which is no surprise—Elise drinks even less than I do.

"Besides," I say as I reach into the green cooler beside the keg and fish through the melting ice until I find two sodas, "it looks like we haven't missed much, huh?"

The party at Jeff's was supposed to start at eight. It's after eleven now. The pounding music was deceiving from outside. Inside the house, things are pretty sedate. I doubt anything exciting happened before we arrived.

We didn't plan on being quite this late; it just sort of ended up that way. Thanks to an instructor who was either incompetent or simply didn't give a shit, Elise's CPR re-cert was over in about forty-five minutes. So she called me to pick her up as soon as she was finished. We strapped the snowshoes back on and hit some of the state land trails that we hadn't been to in a while. Like always, we completely lost track of how late it was and didn't even make it back to the Jeep until well after ten.

Ash shrugs slowly and grins. His cheeks are windburned bright red from yesterday's race, just like mine. "Count on Jeff to have a party that's terminally low-key, right? A bunch of dudes sitting around getting wasted—I think there's like three chicks here or something."

Beside me, I feel Elise bristle, probably at Ash's choice of female terminology. Thankfully, she doesn't say anything.

We skipped dinner, and I'm starved. I open the fridge and browse around. "Speaking of chicks, where's yours tonight?" I ask over my shoulder.

Ash snorts. "Who knows? If I'm lucky, maybe under a snowplow or something." He launches into a diatribe on his recent difficulties trying to get sufficient put-out from his flavor of the week. This is an old song for Ash, and I don't pay much attention.

Elise is looking less and less impressed. She's never been one of Ash's biggest fans, and he's probably offending her feminist sensibilities or something. She leans over the fridge door and whispers, "I'm going to the living room," then takes off.

I find a block of cheddar, slam the refrigerator shut, and break into Ash's pity party. "Hey, congrats on your time, by the way. I didn't get the chance to tell you yesterday."

"Thanks. I was pretty damned close behind Jeff this time. I think I'll be able to take him before the season is out."

"Think so?" He just might. Jeff's the better skier in a technical

sense, but Ash wants it more. Jeff doesn't care about winning
quite as much as he should.

"Pretty shitty news about Cabot, isn't it?" Ash says.

"What news?" I hadn't hung around long enough to hear.

"Looks like he actually ruptured the damn tendon this time—
has to have surgery this week, then probably a shitload of rehab.
In any case, he's down for the season."

I bite a chunk of cheese off the block. "Thank God. He should
have been out weeks ago. He's been trying his damnedest to screw
the whole team up out there."

Ash raises his eyebrows and laughs. "That's a bit harsh, Raff,
don't you think? He is our friend, after all. Yeah, he probably
should have bowed out a couple weeks ago, but we're still doing
fantastic this year. And Cabot's always been solid up to now,
wouldn't you say?"

"Maybe. Not that it matters," I add. "Everyone turns out to be
a disappointment sooner or later, right?"

Ash laughs again, used to hearing this from me. He continues,
"Anyway, at least he's just a junior, so he's still got next year to ski.
That would have sucked for him if he'd missed out on everything
during senior year."

"Yeah, poor guy. Gets to sit on his ass for a few months. Life's
so freaking rough." When someone cares as little about their
effect on the rest of their team as Cabot obviously did, it's hard
to imagine that not being able to ski will mean a hell of a lot to
him.

"You know what I mean." Ash draws another beer for himself and downs at least three-quarters of it without stopping.
"Anyway, I know he felt really bad about not finishing yesterday.

When they were hauling him off to the hospital, he told Jeff to tell you he was sorry. Some of the guys are going down to visit him after practice tomorrow. You interested?"

"Don't know. I'll see what's going on." I already know I'm not interested. Cabot isn't doing me or anyone else any good sitting in some hospital bed. In any case, he'll probably be back home in a week, so what's the point? "Where's Jeff, anyway?" I ask. I don't remember seeing him when I came in.

"Not sure. Saw him about a half hour ago, I think. I'm sure he and Angie are around here somewhere." Ash jumps down from the counter. "Think I'll go see," he says, heading out of the kitchen. "You coming?"

"Be right there," I tell him. I make a stop off at the bathroom in the back hallway, then head back to the living room.

When I get there, I spot Elise sitting on a couch in an alcove at the far end of the huge room, facing away, head bent over some coffee-table book in her lap. She's clearly in her own little world and seemingly oblivious to everything around her. I start to head over to see what she's reading, but Ash's voice stops me.

"Raff—you've gotta check this shit out!"

He's waving me over to where he's standing with McNeal, next to a little den right off the Chadbourns' living room. The door is just barely open and their eyes are glued to something happening inside. As I join him and glance in, the mystery of Jeff's where-abouts is immediately solved.

Through the doorway, I can see that Angelica Pershing, Jeff's girlfriend, has once again proved that she can't quite hold her alcohol like a big girl. She's sprawled on a futon in the corner of the den like a pile of overcooked, overdressed spaghetti. Her blond hair's all over the place, and her left eye's just slightly open, which is a little freaky, if you ask me. For Angie to end a night of partying this way isn't exactly unheard-of, so that's not what we're staring at. It's Jeff.

Generally, Jeff's party-going experience ends with him staying sober enough to play babysitter to Angie. But it looks like he's finally had one too many nights of holding her head over the toilet or making sure she doesn't take her shirt off in public. For once, he's clearly as drunk as Angie is, and he doesn't seem to care that she's halfway out of her clothes.

In fact, he appears to be helping her along. Angie's down to her purple lace bra now, her shirt in a pink heap under Jeff's elbow, and they're all over each other and rapidly heading lower.

"Shit, would you look at that?" I say. I'm admittedly surprised. From her, yes, I'd expect this, but going public with his sex life is not at all shy Jeff's style. He must be really obliterated to be going at it like that. This should prove interesting when he sobers up.

At least he's in his own house.

And at least the evening didn't turn out to be a total bore.

Ash doubles up laughing. "Bitch is horny as hell even when she's wasted, huh?"

McNeal's camera phone flashes. "Come on, Jeff—give her what she wants!"

In the den, Jeff looks over his shoulder at us for a second, maybe surprised to see that he's got an audience. But he's too far gone for it to really register.

"I think they can take it from here," I say, pulling the door shut. A glimpse was funny, sure, but the least I can do is give Jeff some privacy if they decide to get down to any serious business.

"Hey guys, what's up?" Shit. Elise is standing next to us.

"Nothing," I say quickly. I put my arm around her and casually turn her away from the door. Even drunk, McNeal has the presence of mind to stick his phone back in his pocket. Over Elise's head, he gives me a *what now?* look.

Ash, unfortunately, is untroubled by matters of subtlety. "Come here, Elise," he slurs, waving her over. "You can totally hear through the door!"

"Hear what?" Elise looks confused. "Angie was in there a couple minutes ago—I brought her some water. She seemed pretty out of it."

"Well, it sure sounds like she's getting back into it now!" Ash says, cracking himself up.

"Dane, what's going on?" Elise is staring up at me now, confusion turning to suspicion. Before I can answer or stop her, she shrugs off my arm and pushes open the door to the den. Her face goes pale, then flushed.

I've seen that look before.

In a second, she's through the door, closing it behind her. Ash, McNeal, and I stare at one another, then jockey for the nearest spot. We didn't need to bother. Elise's angry voice cuts cleanly through the oak.

"Jeff, what are you doing? Get off her!"

I can't hear Jeff's reply or anything else from inside. I wait about a minute, but when the door stays shut I push my way through after her.

Angie's curled on her side in one corner of the futon, a blanket now covering her lower half. She looks either asleep or passed out.

She sounded pissed from outside, but now Elise just looks

sad. She's down on one knee, eye to eye with Jeff. He blinks his bloodshot eyes, like he's trying to remember who she is. They're both kneeling on the floor now, and she's talking to him in a low, steady whisper that I can't make out. Her hands grip Jeff's upper arms and he can't look away from her.

Suddenly, this has serious embarrassment potential, not to mention being irritating as hell. Not only has Elise made a raging big deal about nothing and broken up the only amusing thing that's happened since we arrived, but now she's got Jeff staring at her like some love-struck cow. With my friends fucking watching through the now-open doorway, I might add. So I quickly intercede, grabbing Elise's shoulder and pulling her to her feet, back out of the den, and over to a corner of the living room before this gets any more out of hand.

"Elise, what do you think you're doing?"

"Stopping Jeff. Let go of me." Elise's brown eyes are wide and snapping fire as she tries to pull out of my grip. I tighten my fingers and take a quick glance over my shoulder. Jeff's watching us in a confused way, but then he looks back at Angelica still lying there like a doorstop and seems to remember who it is that he's here with. Good.

When I don't let go, Elise drops her voice to a low hiss. "Dane, she's drunk. She doesn't have a clue what's going on. You think it's okay to let Jeff do it with her like this?"

"You missed the first part, Lise. Angie's the one who started it."

"I don't care. She's out of it now."

"She wouldn't care, anyway."

"That's not the point! You know everyone's going to find out about this."

"What business is it of mine? Or yours, for that matter?"

"Jeff's your friend. And he's completely wasted, too. You know he's never treated any girl like this."

No, Jeff's always just let himself get pussy-whipped by whomever he gets tangled up with. It's about time he started growing a set, and I'm not about to be the one to stop him. "Jeff's a big boy. He doesn't need you to be his mommy. So give it a rest."

Behind us, Ash has pushed the door to the den shut again. "Go to it, buddy," he calls through it, rapping his knuckles twice against the wood.

Elise sees and starts to turn away. I pull her back to face me. "What's the big deal, anyway?"

She glares at me. "The big deal is that this is getting pretty damned close to rape, Dane."

Rape? "Not really. If neither of them knows what's happening, then where's the problem?"

Elise yanks her arms free. "You're telling me this seems all right to you?" She stares at me like I'm something she just discovered growing on the back of her toilet tank, then starts to walk away.

I've had about enough. Rape? Give me a break. The chick's his girlfriend, for one thing, and she's all over him whenever she gets the chance, anyway, drunk or sober. And she's a pretty annoying bitch in the first place. I know for a fact she doesn't mean anything special to Elise. I grab her wrists again, harder this time. "Why do you care?"

"Why do you *not* care?" Elise's dark eyes are furious.

"Because it doesn't concern me. Or you," I add. "They'll both sleep it off, and nobody will remember a thing in the morning.

It's not Jeff's fault that Angie couldn't finish what she started. Hell, she can embarrass herself this much without Jeff's help. So you're just going to leave it alone, okay? Don't embarrass me anymore." This needs to end soon, before I get any angrier than I already am.

Elise stares at me, her eyes going wet and shiny. Great, here comes the crying bit. I swear girls pull that shit just to piss you off.

But she doesn't cry. She stops trying to push me away and goes sort of limp. She leans her head back against the wall. "Don't you ever feel anything for anyone?"

Yes, I do. Right now I'm feeling pissed at the person I'm supposed to have fun with. But she looks resigned now, and I don't think she'll try to make a scene again. I'm sick of this stupid conversation, anyway.

"Look, I'm going to join the party again. When you've got yourself together, why don't you do the same?" I let go of her and walk through the living room and back to the kitchen for another soda. Ash cocks an eyebrow at me as I go by. I shake my head in response, rolling my eyes.

I get my soda and the cheese I left behind earlier and rejoin Ash, who's now migrated to a couch by the wall. "What was that all about?" he asks.

"Nothing important." I glance back across the room to the closed door. "How do you think our boy did?"

Ash chuckles. "Outdid himself, I'm sure. I didn't know Jeff had it in him," he says fondly. He's pretty drunk by now, too. "What was up with Elise?"

"Nothing." I just want to forget about that. If I think too much about it, I'll get pissed again, and I came out tonight to chill.

"Where'd she go?" Ash asks.

"Go?" I look over to where I left Elise. She's disappeared. So has her parka, which was lying on the couch, and her boots that were by the door. "I don't know."

"She walked out while you were in the kitchen. Think she left?"

"Who knows?" If she did, she's got a two-mile walk ahead of her, since the keys are in my pocket. If she's still wound up, she could probably do with a walk to cool her off, anyway.

And that's one way to solve the problem.

Removing an environmental stressor makes life on the rest of the organisms a lot less of a hassle.

FLORIDA

March 24 , 1:07 a.m.

The moon just slipped behind the bank of clouds that has been rolling in for the past hour. I can't get to sleep. Probably because thinking about Elise has annoyed me. It's amusing, though. Here she got herself all worked up on behalf of some random girl she barely even knew, much less liked. Even fought with me about it.

But when it came to me, she didn't seem quite so concerned, did she?

It proves a good point, though. People always disappoint you. That's why you can't ever be enough of a moron to let yourself give a damn in the first place.

March 27, 1:29 p.m.

"Ow! Jesus, Costello! You trying to kill me?"

Joel doesn't let up, just keeps cranking on my elbow. "Sorry, Dane. You know we've got to do this. You want me to stop for a sec?"

I clench my teeth against the pain. "No. Go ahead."

I've had therapy with Joel for about four days now, and I've never been so sore in my life. Like I've said, his job's to get my arms working again so I can actually start using them.

Recovery from Guillain-Barré is a strange process. After you get to the totally helpless point and hang out there for a while, the whole thing begins to reverse itself. Your body starts laying down a new coating of fat over all your nerves (apparently that's what lets the movement messages get down the neuronal freeways from your brain to your muscles) but at a maddeningly slow pace. Trouble is, during all that time when you can't move, your joints start to tighten up, so by the time you can actually tell your muscles to move on their own, the joints may be too stiff to let it happen.

That's where Joel comes in. Every day he spends an hour pushing, pulling, and twisting on my arms and shoulders, trying to keep them moving until I can do it on my own. And if that sounds easy, allow me to shed some light your way. It hurts like a son of a bitch. It takes all I've got to get through the hour without screaming, although I'd never admit it to Joel.

Joel's cool, though. He doesn't let up, but I know he'd stop if I told him to. I'm just too damned stubborn to give in and tell him to back off.

Because I've got to get moving again, and now that I know therapy can actually be of some use to me, I'm all for it. Absolutely everything in my future's hinging on it. I'm a realist, so I know this ski season's shot for me, but I have to be back in training by the summer if I'm going to be in any kind of condition for the fall. I'm still waiting to hear back on my applications, so I don't know which school I'm going to decide on. But no matter where I go, I'll need to be ready to train as soon as the fall semester starts. Plus, I can't even leave this hellhole until I'm somewhat functional again.

And since I can't even wipe my own ass, that seems like a hell of a ways off.

But it's starting to come back. A little. My hands are tight as hell, but if I really concentrate, I can open and close them about halfway now. Same with my elbows. Once I get the motion back, we'll start strengthening and actually doing stuff.

"Fuck!" Now Joel's doing that awful thing he calls a joint mobilization, but it feels more like he's trying to tear my shoulder off my body. For a little guy, he's freaking strong. I suck in air with a hiss and close my eyes.

"You okay?"

I nod.

"Sure?"

"Just get it over with."

"Almost done, okay? Let me quick do the other side." He

switches arms and starts the process all over again. As usual, he chats while he's torturing me to try to distract me from the fact that he's using me as a human wishbone. I suspect that this physical rehab stuff got its start way back in some medieval dungeon.

He finishes up and leaves my room, returns with two ice bags, and slaps them on my shoulders. After an hour of agony, the beautiful numbness that the cold sends into my twanging muscles and screaming joints feels better than any sensation I can think of. Sex included.

Joel sits down in the bedside chair, which isn't usual. Generally he leaves to get another patient started while I chill down, but his schedule must be light today. "Did I beat you up too much?" he asks.

"I'm fine. Really," I add when he doesn't look completely convinced. "No pain, no gain, right?"

"That's true only up to a point," he says. "I want to get your arms moving, not kill you."

I laugh. "That's good. For a second, I thought you liked to take out your frustrated sexual energies on your helpless patients." One of my ice packs slides off my shoulder.

Joel replaces it, laughing. "No, I run marathons for that. But really," he says, "you're doing great with your OT, Dane. I know it's a lousy process to have to go through. You're tough."

It feels weird to be praised for something that seems so inconsequential. It's not like I've even done anything yet—I just let Joel do his thing without wimping out on him.

He continues, "If you keep up like this, by next week we'll probably be getting into some stuff that's actually functional, like feeding yourself."

"Thank God." That'll be no small relief. The feeding tube

came out of my stomach yesterday, but all that means is that I get to endure an extra fifteen minutes of Letitia pretending a spoon's a damned airplane (complete with dive-bombing sound effects) as she feeds me pureed shit. Apparently my swallowing muscles aren't yet reliable enough to handle anything that isn't the disgusting consistency of Cream of Wheat.

I've been wondering about something else for a couple days now. "When are we going to start working on my legs?" My arms are moving better now, but my lower half still feels tight as ever. Lately, it even seems to have gotten worse instead of better.

"Have they been bothering you?"

"Yeah. I could move my ankles a little last week, but now I can't do it anymore. And they hurt a lot, too."

Joel doesn't seem surprised. "That sounds about right. Your Achilles tendons are probably starting to contract from being in bed all the time."

"Then shouldn't we be doing something about it?" Joel's acting like this is no big deal. "This is my only pair of legs we're talking about, here."

Joel shrugs. "Something should definitely be done about it, Dane, but your legs aren't in my jurisdiction."

"What the hell's that supposed to mean? Are you my therapist or not?"

"It means that I'm an upper-extremity guy. OTs work on fine-motor control—the stuff that comes from your hands, you know? The other stuff—your torso strength, legs, balance—all the stuff that goes into getting you on your feet again? That's the PT realm. Basically, I can help you hold the ski poles, but the PT will get you back on the skis."

I count to ten *slowly* before I respond. "You mean Anya, don't you?"

"She is your PT. Haven't you guys been working together? I know she's been coming in here every day." Joel's a lousy liar. I can tell by his face that he knows perfectly well how Anya and I have been working together.

The news that my legs are seizing up because that bitch hasn't been doing her job seriously pisses me off, and I say as much.

Joel raises his eyebrows. "I don't know what to tell you, Dane," he says, sliding the ice packs off my shoulders. "Anya's been in to see you every day, and I can't think of much more she could do besides that. She's not in the habit of forcing therapy on people who don't want it. Neither am I. Ultimately, it's your choice."

Joel talks some more, but I've pretty much stopped listening. I'm thinking about the choice words I'm going to have for Anya the next time she stops by my room. Hope she's ready to get ripped a new one.

March 28, 10:03 a.m.

"Don't try to pin that on me. It's your own damned fault." Anya spits her words at me, blue eyes flashing.

"Excuse me? How exactly is it my fault that you didn't do your own job?" I can't believe this girl. She's lucky I can't get out of bed.

Anya crosses her arms and leans against the wall. "Didn't do my job? In case you had a brain lapse or something, I've been coming here every day for over a week trying to get started with your PT. Maybe you were too busy playing tough boy and ordering me out of your room to listen. I've also told you what would happen to your legs if you wouldn't let me work with you. I don't know why simple cause and effect is so difficult for you to comprehend."

Her red hair swings forward over her shoulders, framing a face full of freckled satisfaction. Smug bitch.

"So you're saying you're ready to get to work now?" she asks.

I open and close my hands into their half fists. "Are you always this big a pain in the ass?"

"That's another thing. I don't appreciate the attitude you've been pulling with the staff. If we're going to work together, that's the first thing that'll stop."

"Who the hell are you to tell me how I can act? I'm paying to be here!" This crap is absolutely unbelievable. Who does she think she is, the Behavior Police? "Here's the bottom line, princess. I'll do and say whatever the hell I feel like, and you'll do what you're getting paid for. Got it?"

Anya snorts. "Hardly. Nobody here's getting paid enough to put up with any immature crap from you."

"You little—"

She cuts me off. "Look, I know you're in a rotten situation, but you're not going to take it out on me or anyone else here. First off, I won't put up with it, but it also won't help you any. You may not like it, but there's only one way out of here for you. You want to put your own clothes on and wipe your own butt, you have to work with Joel. You want to walk again, you work with—and listen to—me. And we both are here to give you all the help we can. But nobody's getting paid to sit around and wait for you to decide if we're worth your time. My time's valuable, too, and I tend to give it to the people who want to get better and who aren't afraid to work for it."

Me, afraid to work for something? Yeah, right. "Then I'll get a different PT. I'm sure there's another one working here."

"Yes, there's Tom. He's a new graduate who was hired three months ago. You want to be his first shot at taking on a GBS rehab?"

Fuck.

Anya drops her voice back to a normal level, trying to pretend she never lost her cool in the first place. "Look, Dane, it's your choice. Tell me you don't want me here and I'll walk out the door. You can check out my ass one last time, then I'll never come bother you again. It doesn't really matter to me, because my legs work just fine. I can help you, I'd like to help you, and I'm the best shot you have at walking out of here, but I'm not going to take any bullshit doing it."

She walks over to the bed and kneels so we're eye to eye. "Your choice."

If I could think of any possible way to tell her to go to hell I'd gladly take it, but I know when I'm up against a wall. Anya's about the last person I want a symbiosis with, but she's got something and I need it. It's that simple. For now, I'm out of options.

It takes all the strength I've got and it takes forever, but I slide my hand forward to meet the one she's holding out. "Then let's get busy." My voice is cold but reasonably polite.

"Dane," Anya says, letting go of my hand but not getting up, "we just have to work together. Nobody said we have to like each other."

March 30, 8:30 a.m.

Someone tell me this isn't really my life. Yet another morning of fun with Letitia. And I'm once again making small talk to try and forget that I'll be naked in about two minutes.

"What's the deal with the guy across the hall?"

Letitia looks at me like I've suddenly sprouted another head. "You mean Robert?" she asks.

"I don't know what his name is. You know, the one right across the hall. Looks like he's dead?"

She nods. "That'd be Robert. Why you wanting to know about him?"

"I just do. Why does he look like that?"

Letitia takes a washcloth from the pink plastic tub, strangles most of the water out of it, and washes my face. "He's in a coma, sugar. Or something like it."

"No shit? It doesn't look like he's in a coma."

She snorts. "You think folks in comas look like they show it on television? Trust Letitia. You want to see what a coma looks like, you just take a look over at Robert there."

I'll never admit it to her, but she's right. On TV, people in comas always look like they're just sleeping. "How long's he been like that? What happened to him?"

Letitia unsnaps my high-fashion gown, pulls it off my shoulders, and starts washing the rest of me. "You want I should go telling anyone who's feeling nosy all about you and why you lying in this bed all day?"

"No."

"Okay, then." Subject closed, apparently. She finishes dousing me, then drops a towel over me and rummages in the closet.

"Excuse me, is there any good reason why I'm lying here naked and wet?" I haven't quite figured out why nurses have the mindset that modesty is optional. "Didn't you bring a clean gown in with you?" It's not like she hasn't done this almost every morning for the last two weeks—it's not exactly quantum physics.

Letitia resurfaces from my closet with a handful of actual clothes. My clothes. "Nope. Joel told me you're done wearing those stylish things. Says it's high time you got out of this room, and he's got something planned that you gonna like. But you need clothes to be doing it," she says, coming back and scrubbing me with the towel like she's trying to remove my skin instead of dry it.

"Really?" That's excellent news. Veggie ranch or not, there has to be something better than this room that I've been staring around for two weeks. Even my therapy's been in here. "What are we doing? When?"

She laughs. "Don't know. Maybe tomorrow, maybe today? You ask Joel." Letitia's news puts me in a relatively decent mood, and I don't even bother yelling at her when she accidentally knocks my IV as she unhooks it to pull my shirt over my head, even though it hurts like hell.

When she's finished, Letitia holds up a mirror. "Now don't you look decent, sweet pea?"

With the X-rated, dishwater-gray gown of the past weeks replaced by jeans and a long-sleeved T-shirt, I actually feel more like a human being than a science project, even though my hair's almost long enough for a ponytail and the clothes don't fit quite right. I need to start gaining back all the weight I've lost.

I'm still curious about the guy Robert. And the rest of his family, too, especially the girl with the deerskin braid and the quicksilver temper. I've seen her a couple times since our first encounter, and she's put an inordinate amount of energy into sidelong glares as she passes my doorway. I can't resist one last question. "So Robert just lies there like that all the time? Does he ever say anything?"

"He's not nearly as charming as you, baby, if that's what you mean," Letitia says. "Now I don't know why you being all civil this morning, but it's starting to make me nervous. Why, you ain't even told me what kinda big, round thing I look like today!" She grins, pointing to her plain white scrubs.

I think for a minute. "The *Hindenburg*."

"That's more like it, sugar!" she crows, slapping her knee. "Now, let's see what you got for breakfast." She pulls the tray toward her and takes off the lid. "Hmm. Looks like they pureed up some eggs for you. Glad I ain't the one gotta eat them."

March 30, 1:00 p.m.

"Here we go," Joel says as we head out the sliding door and down the ramp toward the pond path. "Freedom!"

I'm too hypnotized by the feeling of warm wind on my face to even reply.

Joel's surprise turned out to be my first lesson in power wheelchair operation. I wasn't at all sold on the idea at first—after all, I plan on being back on my feet before long—but Joel made a good point. While I'm working on getting back to walking and stuff, why spend any more time stuck inside my room than I have to? If I learn to use the wheelchair for the time being, then I can actually start getting around under my own power, which sounds like a damned good idea to me.

We spent a few minutes practicing inside to let me get a feel for how the thing operates, then Joel decided we should celebrate by heading outside—technically to work on fine-motor control (a.k.a. Can you operate the joystick well enough to avoid plunging off the path into the pond?), but really, I think, to cure what's become my near-terminal case of stir-craziness. For weeks looking out my window's been the only link I've had to the outside world, and Joel's probably gotten sick of dragging my attention back inside during therapy.

Now, as I navigate my chair down onto the path beside the pond, I can taste the wet-cotton air on my lips, hear the trilling of cicadas, the gurgling of bullfrogs, and the splash of a wood stork wading through the shallow water. The heavy breeze against my face smells like citrus and damp, green decay.

And I've suddenly become a part of the world again. The feeling is impossible to describe.

Joel looks over at me and grins. "Feels good to get out, doesn't it?" By now I've learned that he spends every minute outside that he can, which is probably why he wanted to get me out here as soon as I could control the chair. Not that I mind.

"Feels a lot better than good."

We cruise along the path for a while, and Joel rattles off tree names for me. I've never seen anything quite like this Florida flora, which has to take some sort of Weird and Wild Tree award. Tiny trees with waxy, fluorescent flowers bigger than my head. Enormous trees full of sausage-looking fruits hanging off branches from skinny stems, as though a bunch of angry vegans held a mass bratwurst lynching last night. A palm tree with a huge, woody yellow obelisk in its center that sticks up like a giant ear of phallic corn. Listening as Joel tells me about each tree is almost like hearing a story—not only does he know a shitload about this stuff, he also seems to enjoy sharing what he knows and answering my endless questions. My dad would sometimes talk with me like this, but more often he'd just rattle off some long Latin words, then tell me to go look it up if I wanted to know more.

"So, how's PT going?" Joel asks.

I roll my eyes. "Take a guess." Anya and I may have reluctantly agreed to work with each other, but our interactions have fallen short of anything approaching mutually beneficial.

Joel laughs. "Having some growing pains together, are you?"

"More like having to put up with a lot of shit."

"Which one's dishing it out?"

"Like you need to ask?" He has to be putting me on. I'm sure Anya isn't any more of a treat as a co-worker than as a therapist, even if Joel is one of the most good-natured people I've ever encountered.

Joel raises his eyebrows and grins. "Let's just say I imagine the two of you present an interesting challenge to each other." He reaches up and pulls a long tendril of what looks like rotten green gauze from an overhanging conifer branch. "Here, feel that," he says, draping it across my lap. "Spanish moss."

I run my fingers over the feathery strands, which feel a lot softer than they look hanging from the trees. "Wild. Is it a fungus?" Most of the conifers here are cobwebbed with ropes of the strange stuff, and I'd assumed they were affected with some sort of blight.

"Bromeliad. Lives on the tree but won't kill it."

My thoughts go back to Anya, even though she's a lot less interesting than bromeliads *or* fungus. "I'm giving *her* a challenge? How the hell can I do that? If I so much as look at her cross-eyed, she slaps me onto that goddamned tilt table and leaves me there!"

I'm referring to an incident of two days' past, when Anya strapped me onto this table contraption that can be cranked from horizontal to completely vertical, bringing the person on it along like Frankenstein's monster rising from the slab. Supposedly, being upright and putting weight on your feet is good for your bones and joints, even if you can't do it yourself, so Anya's had me on it for a few minutes every day, until my ankles start to hurt from being stretched so much. It also makes you dizzy if you do it for too long at first.

But the other day we got to arguing about something or other while she was putting me on it. I apparently said something that offended her because she cranked the damned thing all the way up and left the room. Witch came back twenty minutes later and let me down like nothing had happened, even though my ankles felt like they'd been put on a rack, my legs were shaking, and I was so lightheaded I felt nauseous. I guess she thought she was making some profound point. All it did was piss me off.

Joel isn't surprised when I tell him. "Yeah, Anya told me about that," he says. It figures that she would have jabbered to him.

"Do you therapists gossip about all your patients?"

"We prefer to call it exchanging pertinent clinical information. Sounds more official."

"Uh-huh. Cute." We roll along in silence for a few minutes, following the path as it winds through a thick stand of prehistoric-looking banyan trees, then doubles back toward the pond. I'll say this for the place—it has some nice grounds. Joel said the whole complex covers at least three hundred acres.

"Seriously," I ask after a bit. "She must be a profound ass-ache as a co-worker. Are the rest of the therapists here any better?" I know there's at least one other PT and OT who work here, but I've met only Joel and Anya, since they're the ones who treat me.

We come to a wooden bench and Joel sits down, stretching out his legs and folding his arms. "Better than Anya?" he says kind of absently as he squints out over the water. "Absolutely not."

God, if everyone else here is *worse* to be around than the Glacial Princess, I have no idea how Joel manages to stay sane. I start to offer my condolences but stop when I notice a funny expression on his face. And realize why.

"You have a thing for her, don't you?"

Joel doesn't deny it, just shrugs slowly and deliberately. The look on his face changes from distant into something else, and I know I'm right.

This one completely blows me away. Joel's so … cool. Chill. Someone you actually don't mind talking to. And Anya? She's wound so tight I'll bet she never even farts without it freezing on the way out.

"I don't get it. I mean, sure she's got the body of Venus, but isn't that a little offset by her barracuda personality?" I don't care how good-looking a chick is. Without some supporting qualifications, she simply isn't worth the time. Funny—I would have expected Joel to feel the same way.

Joel glances over. "Um, aren't you the one who's always going on about not wanting anyone nosing into your personal affairs? You think maybe this qualifies as my business?"

He's not completely serious. By now, I know that Joel's pretty much an open book. The guy's in a perpetual state of benign good humor. If it was anyone else, that attitude would annoy the hell out of me, but for some reason it's okay when it comes from him. Anyway, I don't know of too many conversational topics that would truly be closed with Joel, so I can push the issue at least a little further.

"Does she know? I mean, have you told her or anything?"

"Hell, no. And don't even think about it," he adds, giving me a look. "Just remember that I'm in charge of half your therapy. Don't think I'll hesitate to put you in severe pain, got it?" He laughs, but it's clear that he's serious about wanting to keep his unspoken worship from afar to himself.

"Are you kidding? You think I talk to her any more than I absolutely have to?" It's bad enough having to see her and try to be somewhat civil while she's torturing me for an hour every day—I'm certainly not going to go looking for things to say to her. "But seriously, Joel, I don't get it. What's the draw?"

He looks amused. "Does it matter? Haven't you ever been hung up on someone before? You have a girlfriend back home?"

An image of Elise, curled asleep under my fleece blanket on the all-night drive home from Walden Pond, flashes in my mind for a microsecond. *You come, too.* I shove it away before I have time to feel anything.

"No."

"No girlfriend, or never been hung up?"

"Both."

Joel stops smiling. "That's too bad."

"What's so great about making yourself nuts over some girl who doesn't even know you exist?"

"Guess I can't explain it. It just is."

"Well if it's so damned wonderful, why haven't you gotten up the balls to do anything about it?"

"Oh, I imagine I'll get up the nerve one of these days."

"But, Joel, she's practically psychotic. She's got a chip on her shoulder you couldn't cut with a chainsaw. What could you possibly be hung up on?" I know Joel's a little strange sometimes, but I really don't understand this.

"I know she comes across that way sometimes, but it's not her fault." Joel sighs, scowls. "Anya was in a really bad relationship a while back."

"So now she takes it out on the world because she's bitter?" Come on, princess, we all have to grow up sometime. "Lots of people get dumped and manage to deal just fine." It's not like it's any big calamity, anyway.

Joel bites his lip, like he seriously buys the old wounded-in-love routine. "We're good friends, but I don't think she's ready to think of me—or probably anyone else—in those terms again."

I feel my estimation of Joel slipping. "I mean, what are we talking about here, anyway? Maybe she got her feelings hurt? Some guy didn't give her enough attention or something?"

Joel raises his eyebrows. "It was a bit more abusive than that" is all he says.

Now, the whole "broken girl" song and dance may be Joel's thing, but it's never done much for me. If you ask me, it's just another excuse some people trot out to justify their dysfunctional behavior.

"I don't buy it, Joel. So she was abused, or whatever. Even if it's true, nobody said she had to stay and put up with it, did they?"

I know it's politically correct to be all horrified and pitying about battered women and such, but when a girl sits there and lets things happen to her, it makes me think even less of her. It's exactly like the whole thing back in New York with Angelica and Jeff.

"How can you have respect for someone who doesn't even respect herself?" I add.

And suddenly, it's like a shade's been yanked down behind

Joel's eyes. His normally open and cheerful face disappears like a fading chameleon, replaced by an expressionless blank.

Joel stands up. "I think we're done for today."

"But we've only been out here half an hour!" PT and OT are usually at least an hour each. Besides, I haven't been outside like this in way too long.

"We're done," Joel repeats, just as quietly as before. Without looking at me, he reaches over and flicks the joystick on my chair, spinning me around.

"Hey!" I protest as Joel strides up the path back toward the building, propelling my chair along with him, even though I can do it myself. "What's the deal?"

He doesn't stop or look at me, just keeps hauling me alongside. "If you don't know, then nothing I can say will make any impression."

March 30, 1:45 p.m.

So I'm back in my room, screwed out of a rightfully deserved half hour of outside time. Instead, I'm yet again watching through the window as the alligator in the pond stalks two egrets. After we got back inside, Joel left with barely a word, which for him is a one-eighty personality switch. I guess he was really pissed. And he took my wheelchair with him.

It's weird seeing him mad when he's usually so laid-back. And it feels strangely uncomfortable to know it's me he's pissed at. I generally don't pay attention to people and their dumb little mood swings and other histrionics.

Truthfully, I'm a little annoyed with him, too. What the hell did he mean with that if-you-don't-know-then-why-should-I-tell-you line? It's the same thing Elise used to pull on me, acting like I was missing some big, obvious point she thought should be crystal clear.

You know, she accused me of never listening, never thinking about what she said. That's not true. Can I help it that I choose to do most of my thinking—like just about everything else that's important—alone?

UPSTATE NEW YORK

February 12, 1:58 a.m.

It's almost two in the morning when I finally leave the party. The Jeep's windows are thoroughly frozen, so I spend an intimate ten minutes with my ice scraper before I can get going. This might have been more pleasant were it not zero degrees and windy, and if I hadn't left my gloves in my gym bag on my bed. Oh, well— you screw up, you pay for it. I'll remember next time.

I'm not even that tired, but things at Jeff's were pretty dead. Everyone who wasn't passed out had started salivating over a baggie full of happy mushrooms, and any chance of coherent conversation was taking an exponential nosedive. People say getting high gives them clarity, or some such shit, but in most cases it sure doesn't make them any less boring to talk to. Anyway, the whole scene was turning into a big waste of time.

I don't go in much for the chemically induced pseudo-enlightenment, myself, whether smoked or imbibed. I think it was Ernest Hemingway who said that intelligent people sometimes need to drink in order to tolerate fools. An intriguing theory, and I certainly tested it once or twice. But it ended up a no-go, for three reasons. For one, people really *aren't* much more interesting or tolerable, regardless of my location on the sheets-to-the-wind

spectrum. Second, I get a far superior rush from catching sight
of the northern lights from my canoe, or barreling through the
Nordic run when it's untouched after a fresh snowfall, than from
staring down a bottle of cheap, weasel-piss-tasting beer. Third—
and not at all least—I can't think of a single bigger waste of a day
than nursing a cranium-splitting hangover.

And considering that Hemingway blew his brains out despite
his clever human-relations theory, I guess it wasn't such a success
for him, either.

Unfortunately, I guess there isn't any effective way to make
most people interesting. Maybe that's why I rarely bother trying.

I should have taken off from Jeff's sooner than this—I'm going
to be cursing myself in the morning (later morning, I should say)
when I'm dragging my dead ass through a workout. Oh, well. I'll
be able to perform, regardless—just may need a nap afterward.

I don't even mind that I'll feel like crap when 6:00 a.m. rolls
around. I can bet, though, that half my team will put in a half-
assed practice tomorrow because of tonight's alcoholic stupor. I
don't care if you want to mess yourself up, but do it on your own
time.

Don't waste mine, for God's sake.

The sun did make it out for a while earlier in the day, but now
the clouds have started to roll back in and a light snow is falling.
It hasn't been going on long enough to mess up the streets yet,
and I'm cruising over the back roads at a pretty decent clip as I
head home. Even with the clouds, enough moonlight is reflecting
off the snow already on the ground to light things up pretty good.
It's just bright enough that I've killed my headlights.

I love doing that. Driving through the darkness with no

synthetic illumination as a buffer between me and the road. The lights take something away from what you see; they put a sharp glaring edge on everything that's never truly in focus. I think they just get in the way, for the most part.

So sometimes I get rid of them.

I'm getting to the turnoff that leads to my road. I brake for the turn, then change my mind and accelerate past it, farther down into the huge tracts of state forest surrounding the scattered pockets of houses.

I need to think.

The state road I turn off on is dirt and obviously not a winter hot spot with the rangers—it looks like it hasn't been plowed since around November.

I switch over to four-wheel, then slowly negotiate the packed ice and slush that's drifted over the road, a couple feet high in some places. One miscalculation or overcompensation or stray tap on the brake and I'll end up in the ditch. But driving in snow's not that much different from skiing on it. You just have to know where you are, where you want to be, and the most logical way to get the two to link up.

As I get deeper into the woods, the evergreens start blocking out more and more of the moonlight and, much as I hate to, I end up having to switch the headlights back on to see what the hell I'm aiming at. The road dips and winds for another two miles or so, finally emptying itself out into a clearing beside a good-size lake.

I found this place by accident last year, and I've been coming back ever since. Nobody else ever comes here, as far as I can tell. Even the rangers and game wardens never seem to use the road, so I guess it's just been forgotten. But it's a sweet little spot—I spent a good chunk of the summer snorkeling here and got acquainted with most of the regulars, the most interesting of which was a snapping turtle whose carapace had to measure at least three feet across. Got a little too close once, and the giant bastard almost ate my left hand.

Now the lake is glassy, frozen in crazy ripples from the wind and drifted here and there with blowing snow. As I kill the engine and get out, the moon breaks through the clouds, illuminating the clearing and capping trees, snow, and ice with a silver-wash glow. It's still cold as hell out, so cold that the air stings when I inhale and rises like smoke when I breathe out. I grab my parka from the backseat and pull on a pair of lined Carhartt overalls. Now I can at least enjoy the night without freezing my ass off, though I do have to keep my hands in my pockets.

I step carefully onto the ice, making my way toward the middle. If you move your feet like you've got skis on, you're not likely to fall. At the center I stop for a second, then walk in a slowly expanding circle, spiraling back toward the shoreline in concentric arcs. Auriga is barely visible through the break in the clouds overhead, just above the tip of Taurus's horn. It's a little constellation, and hard to make out unless the sky's totally clear, which it rarely is around here—it's just a stroke of luck that that spot is cloudless at the moment.

Elise and I couldn't find it last week when I brought her here. We finally gave up and built a fire, then sat wrapped in sleeping bags with snow landing on our faces. We spent hours talking about Thoreau, debating whether he would have found more inspiration out in a place like this, where he couldn't have broken up his communion with nature with daily walks into town for wine and conversation. Elise was convinced that taking time to get out of the woods, talk to people, and get a quick dose of the civilized world every day would have been a good thing. She insisted that it must have given him a good balance between solitude and community, and that without that interaction, his perspectives and writing would have been too one-sided.

I, on the other hand, think that Thoreau was insane to ever leave his cabin in the woods. He had the intelligence (which is rare enough) and the ability to say something meaningful, the means to live outside of society, and the perfect place to do it. Yet he voluntarily chose to walk to town every day?

If I had a cabin in the woods and was independently wealthy, you'd sure as hell never see me again.

I think about how Elise stormed out tonight, and I'm annoyed. I wish I knew why she pulls shit like this sometimes. I can't quite figure that girl out, just like I can't figure out exactly how I feel about her. We can have such a kick-ass time together, and usually we do. She's smart, pretty, great in bed. Most especially, though, she's up for absolutely everything, and we like doing so many of the same things. I've never dated any other girl who would do anything with me, no matter how weird or spontaneous. Doesn't matter if it's wet, cold, slimy, or dirty, late at night or four in the morning—she's ready to go and she has as good a time as I do.

And when we talk, she listens, but never with the headlight-blinded blank stare most people get when a conversation becomes too cerebral for them. When Elise and I get talking or debating, I can almost see the thoughts bouncing around behind her eyes. And she actually has some interesting things to say, too. That's just not something you find every day.

So why does she have to screw it up with all this other stupid shit? All the crap about caring about each other's needs, and consideration, and all the other two-bit therapy words she pulls out to try and make me feel guilty whenever I won't do some stupid thing or other for her. I don't know what the hell she wants sometimes—we have fun together, for God's sake. We go places, see things, argue literature and science and politics. Why on earth does she have to get in some stupid twist and say I demand too much of people, or don't really listen? I'm more than happy to listen, as long as something interesting and worthwhile is being said.

Sometimes she looks at me like I'm completely missing something. Which is nuts.

And as far as demanding goes, I'm not the one imposing moral standards on someone else.

Like that shit with Angelica tonight. I don't have a clue what she thought *I* should have done back there—that was between Jeff and his girlfriend. And why the fuck should I have pretended I didn't think it was funny? Bottom line, it was. And it would have been funny if it had been the other way around, if Jeff had been the one who passed out first and left Angelica to finish things up.

But Elise always has to go and make it personal, has to make it seem like I'm lacking some idiotic moral code that she thinks everyone in the whole damned world is supposed to know about and follow to the letter. For some reason I've yet to figure out, she's convinced we should all run around looking for ways to help each other out. It's the one manner in which she wastes time. Now, if she wants to do that, fine. I don't mind. But she's got to learn to leave me out of it, because there's no way I'm wasting effort to get some idiot out of a situation he got himself into in the first place.

The wind kicks up as I pace, whirling snow against my face in a fine powder and making the ice-glaze on the leafless trees rattle stiffly. I keep circling.

I mean, if Angelica even cared about it, she wouldn't let herself get that drunk in the first place.

And how does damage control become someone else's responsibility?

The wind kicks up again, harder now. I've circled all the way back to the Jeep. It's getting downright cold.

I get in, crank the engine and the heater, and blow on my numb fingers. Enough of this. There's nothing to discuss, debate, or even think any more about.

If you have that little control over yourself, you don't deserve any help.

End of story.

FLORIDA

March 30, 2:44 p.m.

I don't think about things? Bullshit.

What I don't get is why Joel and Elise—two of the only people whose opinions have even mattered to me—seem to think so.

Damn it.

April 2, 12:05 p.m.

I'm lurking on the concrete apron behind the greenhouses, perhaps the world's first spy with power-wheelchair transport. James Bond would not be impressed.

Here at the veggie ranch, they supposedly use the greenhouses for vocational rehabilitation. I use the term loosely. Apparently, besides trying to physically put people back together, this place attempts to send them off as productive members of society whenever (or if ever) they get out. But for some of the loony birds I see through Joel's binoculars, that day looks to be somewhere over the distant horizon.

At the first row of long benches, some loser in a blue staff polo shirt is demonstrating how to transplant little trees into larger pots, like he isn't aware of the horizontal learning curve of his audience. At another bench, a guy with a huge reddish scar curving across his shaved head, biker tattoos, and his pants on backward is eating the leaves off his banana tree instead of transplanting it. Beside him, a round little grandmother type in a blue muumuu is busy troweling dirt from her pot onto the floor. Almost hidden behind a huge rubber tree in the corner is my old buddy Isaac, resplendent in his top hat and sparkles and decorating a potted palm with several of his fluorescent plastic necklaces.

Granny dumps a load of dirt into Biker Dude's sandal. I can't hear what he says through the window in front of me, but I don't think he's complimenting her aim. I enjoy watching their exchange until Granny bashes him with her pink plastic trowel and the staff guy reaches for his cell phone. Then I abandon the field observations, spin a one-eighty, and make tracks down the path toward the woods on the far side of the pond. Ten to one he's just called for some reinforcements from the mother ship, and the last thing I need is to get caught when they arrive.

I was only supposed to be out and about in the wheelchair for half an hour. Which, according to my watch, makes me exactly thirty-five minutes late. Joel and Anya gave me a line about having to get used to sitting up gradually so it won't overwork my muscles or mess with my blood pressure or some shit. I don't buy it. This chair has so much freaking back support that you couldn't slouch in it if you had no bones. Anyway, we've been going through the same routine for the past three days—I get put into the wheelchair after PT at eleven and Anya reads me the riot act about how the world will end if I don't report back to be stuck in bed by 11:30 for an absolutely essential rest before OT. Forever and ever, amen. I nod seriously like I'm listening, then take off through the automatic doors to the bliss of outdoor freedom.

Then come back whenever I feel like it. Yesterday, I even missed OT, which was supposed to be at one. Joel didn't say too much, but Anya threatened to either sabotage the chair's battery pack or come outside and personally hunt me down if I pulled the same stunt today.

She'll have to find me first.

I buzz along the path, rubber tires humming on the hot asphalt, stopping once to check out an armadillo through the binoculars. Joel's been a little chilly ever since he got pissed at me, but he still lets me use his binoculars every day. And what's better, he rigged up this sweet little stand that attaches right onto the tray of my wheelchair for the binoculars to rest on. So all I have to do to look through them is point the chair at what I want to see, then lean forward a couple inches, which is tiring, but I can manage it for short periods. I've even gotten reasonably good at driving the chair while looking through the binoculars.

The sticky heat of the sun dissolves into shady coolness as I cruise into the shadows of a thick stand of tall, scaly trunked trees. Since I've paid attention to Joel, I can tell they're longleaf pines by their long, brushy needle clusters and the huge, almost spherical cones scattered on the ground beneath them. From somewhere on the path ahead of me comes a rhythmic, repeated *thunking*.

I turn the chair around for a second and look back across the pond to scan the rear of the main building. No sign of angry therapists storming out on a Dane-reconnaissance mission yet. Good. I spin back around and head toward the thunking sound, which sounds pretty aggressive. I find out why when I turn the next bend.

It's the girl from the dead-looking guy's room. Her long hair's in two tight braids instead of one, and she's wearing baggy black shorts and cleats. Today's T-shirt is olive green and features a little cartoon guy sticking out his tongue and squeezing his thumb and forefinger together. *I Care This Much*, it states. She slams a cleat into the soccer ball in front of her, which sends bark flying as it ricochets off a scaly trunk and rebounds to her. She's facing away from me and is too intent on demolishing either the ball or the tree to realize she's got an audience. Until I crack up laughing.

Well, what would you do if you watched someone smash a soccer ball into a tree, only to have the tree retaliate by sending a shower of longleaf pine cones down onto her head? Which, by the way, appear to be bullet-hard, sharp-edged, and absolutely monster-size. No joke—they're almost as big as my hand with the fingers fully spread out (which I can do now, by the way). The progression is perfect: cones fall, they nail her on the head, she yelps, and the soccer ball bounces away into some shrubs. And I laugh.

She spins around and says something insulting, then proceeds to trample three of the cones with her cleats, glaring at me as she stomps. Her skin's darker than you'd expect with the lightness of her brown hair, and her eyes are an odd dusty gray, like campfire ashes.

"Come on," I say, still laughing. "You know it was funny. And it's not like it was the pine cones' fault. Do you really need to take it out on them?"

She doesn't reply, just jumps on them harder.

Something about this girl intrigues me. "Okay," I say. "So now that we've established you don't have a sense of humor, do you at least have a name?"

"Carissa. Not that it's any of your business." She stops jumping, having reduced the cones to shards. "And my sense of humor's just fine, thanks. I only laugh when I find something funny."

She's a treat and a half. "Nice to meet you, Carissa-not-that-it's-any-of-your-business. I'm Dane."

"I know. I read your door. Why'd your parents name you after a dog?"

Like I've never heard that one before. "That the best you can do? Weak." I change to a more interesting subject. "Hey, that guy whose room you're always in—he your dad?"

"He was. Why? Can you think of another reason why I'd be hanging out in some middle-aged guy's hospital room for days on end?"

"What do you mean, 'was'?"

"Does he look particularly dad-like to you at the moment?" Carissa flicks some loose hair back from her sweaty face and goes over to fish her ball out of the shrubs.

She's got a point. "Then why are you here all the time?"

Carissa backs out of the bushes with the recovered ball. "You'll have to refer that question to my lovely mother," she says. "I sure as hell don't have anything to do with this life choice."

"What happened to him, anyway?" I ask.

"I could have guessed you'd be unoriginal as well as nosy."

All right, the tough-girl insults were marginally cute for a while, but enough's enough. "Why are you so pissed off all the time? I just asked a simple question."

"A nosy one. Your knowing what happened to my dad isn't going to change anything. He'll still be exactly the way he is. So," she says, bouncing the ball a couple times on the asphalt path, "your question is purely nosy. Not to mention completely pointless."

"At least I'm smart enough to know what'll happen if you kick a ball against a tree full of cones."

"At least I can kick a ball," she counters, eyeing my wheelchair.

Bitch.

"Now I'll think of some nosy questions to ask you." Carissa drops the soccer ball and picks up a few of the remaining untrampled pine cones, which she proceeds to juggle.

"If you want to know what landed me here, you can look it up," I say to head off her interrogation. "Under 'Guillain-Barré Syndrome,' if you can spell it." The huge pine cones arc through the air in sequence, barely missing one another as they fly between her hands. Watching the fluid way her body moves—the way it *works*—is starting to irritate me. I had wanted to get a closer look at one of those cones, and I'm tempted to ask her to get one for me. But I sure as hell won't.

"I couldn't care less what your problem is, to be perfectly honest," Carissa says. "What I want to know is how your family managed to make sure your problem didn't become theirs."

"Like you know anything about my family. They're all back in New York."

"Exactly." Carissa flips one of the pine cones onto my wheelchair tray, which narrowly misses the binocular stand Joel set up and spins in a few circles before coming to a stop. She keeps the other three in the air without missing a beat. It was far from an act of altruism—she was just showing off—but at least I got the cone I wanted.

"And I think that's great," she goes on. "At least they're not wasting any of their own lives hanging around this human junkyard." She jerks her head back in the direction of the main building.

No, they certainly aren't. I angle my chair toward a break in the trees, then lean forward and stare through the binoculars again. Maybe something interesting will wander by before too long.

"But they probably call you all the time and stuff, right?" Carissa stops juggling and looks at me. "I mean, that's a smart way to do it. They don't feel guilty and you're out of their way."

My parents call all the time? That's hilarious. Dad did phone back once after my idiotic call—to let me know that he's got me enrolled in summer school. In order to start college on time in the fall, I'll have to make up the last half of senior year during the summer session, which starts the last week in May. That should give me plenty of time to finish up with rehab, get home, and be ready to start training.

But in the meantime, I'm still stuck here. Being insulted by some girl who can't control her temper and who has nothing better to do than psychoanalyze my family.

"Why would I want them here in the first place?" I counter, still looking through the binoculars. "It's not like I'm going to be here that long—just until I get back on my feet again."

Carissa raises her eyebrows. "Back on your feet?" she says doubtfully, looking me over. "You sure you know what you're talking about? I'll admit that you don't seem *quite* as mentally deranged as most of this fruitcake circus, but you still look like hell."

Like hell? Who does this chick think she's talking to?

"And not to state the obvious," she continues, "but you're driving a wheelchair around."

I look up from the binoculars at that one. "Brilliant, Holmes. What the fuck's your point?"

"Doesn't that mean you broke your back or something? And that you'll probably be stuck like that forever?"

That's it. I'm out of here. Insulting me is one thing, but now she's showing her stupidity, and I have far better ways to spend my time than sitting here listening to that crap.

"You know, you should watch yourself." My voice is cold enough to plummet the heat-hazy air into frostbite range. "You go around broadcasting that you're a cerebral derelict, and someone might think you belong here." I spin my chair around, careful to rest my arm on the pine cone to keep it from falling off the tray, and take off up the path the way I came in before she can say anything else. Or perhaps try and figure out what *derelict* means.

I stop when I emerge from the trees by the pond. Across the water, back at the main building, I glimpse a flash of red hair. I look through the binoculars and see Joel and Anya heading down the ramp together. I check my watch: 12:29. They should be on their lunch break now. Is Anya actually planning on following through with her threat? If she is, I'm not going to make it easy on her.

I flip into reverse and back slightly into the shadow of the trees behind me. They probably can't see me from this far away, especially since I have Joel's binoculars. I watch them as they walk across the lawn and into one of the maintenance sheds.

This could be fun. I have the advantage of the binoculars, and this chair cruises pretty quickly. They'll have a hard time even finding me, much less catching me when I've already got this much of a head start on them. And my battery pack was fully charged right before I came out, so I've got plenty of power left in the chair.

Truthfully, I'm already a little disappointed in their strategy. Why on earth would they think I'd be in the maintenance shed?

Speaking of the shed, something's happening over there. One

of the automatic doors is creaking open. Two people come into view.

It's Joel and Anya.

In a golf cart.

Anya's driving.

Shit.

April 2, 12:37 p.m.

Okay, so I got busted.

After the cavalry escorts me back to the gulag, I go back to my room, more to escape Anya's tirade than to get ready for OT.

There's a letter lying on my bed.

I've never gotten too excited about mail one way or the other and generally agree with Thoreau's opinion about letters—almost nothing of interest or value comes in them, and the vast majority of them aren't even worth the postage. So it's odd that I find myself rushing over to the bed, actually excited to see what it is and who it's from.

There's no name on the return address, but I recognize the messy handwriting as my brother's.

There's no logical reason why I should be disappointed to hear from Eric. Maybe some stupid part of me was thinking that it would be from Elise. She always was a champion letter writer. Never could agree with me that they were unnecessary.

It doesn't matter, anyway.

I can't even pick up the envelope, of course, much less open it. So, just like with everything else that I want to do, I'll have to wait for Letitia to do it for me later. In the meantime, I'd better get my ass down to OT so I can hurry up and learn how to do things myself.

I wonder how Eric's been doing since I left. Probably better actually, now that I'm not around to set standards that he could never match. It's probably easier for him without me there.

UPSTATE NEW YORK

February 13, 3:39 p.m.

"Hold it steady," Dad shouts over the growl of the chain saw. I brace my feet on the frozen road and grip the narrowest part of the tree trunk as the saw gnaws slowly through the wood.

Today's father-son bonding takes the form of North Country home maintenance. A freak ice storm blew through last night, and that always means big fun for homeowners everywhere across our fair northern land. This one was a little guy—nothing like the one years back that ripped down telephone poles and knocked out our power for two weeks—but it still left a few inches of ice on things and took down some lines and a couple trees. Dad and I spent most of the morning smashing through the frozen glaze coating the roof of our house, and now we've moved on to the good-size poplar that toppled under the weight of the ice clinging to its branches. It's blocking the road and since we live pretty far out of the way, it'll probably be a while before the road crews make it back here. So we're disposing of it ourselves.

The fact that we're even out here is amusing. Dad could easily afford to hire someone to come in and get this done for us. But he's funny about things like that. He takes some sort of pride in doing all the manual labor around our place by himself (and with me when I get roped into it, which seems to happen often). It's like he has to periodically prove to the world or himself that he hasn't forgotten his blue-collar roots.

That probably also explains why we live down a dirt road in a big old farmhouse. Forget that it's been completely redone in solid-wood paneling, stained-glass windows, and marble fireplaces, and that the barn's been converted into a state-of-the art woodworking shop that Dad only uses occasionally.

I don't mind, though. I rarely complain about doing anything outside, and I like the time with Dad. Work usually keeps him pretty tied up, and even when he is around, he's not big on quality time that's not productive in some way.

I hold my end of the trunk as Dad saws the entire tree into manageable chunks. We smashed the ice crust covering the bark with hatchets before getting started, but it's still slow going. I'm sweating from the hours of work but the air's cold, and our breath rises in steamy curls. He won't let me use the chain saw, even though I've been helping him clear blowdowns since I was eight. He never trusts the skilled work to anyone but himself.

Dad cuts the last branch free and kills the chain saw. "That about does it."

I drop to one knee to gather up an armload of branches. Piece by piece, we haul the small stuff to the woodpile on the back deck, then wrestle the big chunks off the road. These we pile in the old tractor shed to dry out.

I'm beat by the time the road's clear. Guess yesterday's practice took more out of me than I thought. Chalk it up to lack of sleep courtesy of Jeff's party and my predawn visit to the lake afterward.

I look at Dad, waiting for his verdict. He surveys the cleared

road, the now-higher woodpile and the ice-free roof. "Call it a
day?" he says.

I stow the chain saw in the garage and follow him onto the porch to shake off most of the snow that's covering us like sentient snowmen, then into the house.

Which doesn't seem quite as warm as it was when Dad and I came outside a few hours earlier.

Dad notices. "Eric!" he yells.

No answer.

I get out two mugs and start making cocoa while Dad storms into the living room in search of my brother. Sounds like he found him, from the yelling I hear.

Eric doesn't do himself any favors by being such a flake. If you're going to forget to keep the fire going, at least don't hang out in the same room as the fireplace.

Dad comes back into the kitchen, looking pissed. "I don't understand that brother of yours, Dane." He takes the steaming mug I hold out to him and paces around the room. "You were never like this. Is he actually as incompetent as he seems so determined to portray himself?"

I sit down at the table with my cocoa, dragging my spoon through it to melt the marshmallows. I shrug in response to Dad's question that isn't really a question. He's never been happy with Eric for as long as I can remember, and that's been about as long as Eric's been around.

Sadly, my little brother can at best be described as Eric the Average. Unremarkable looks, solid B grades that he really has to work for, no exceptional skills that anyone can call to mind. The one sport he's less than hopeless at is karate, and even there, his girlfriend's a couple belts ahead of him. Talk about embarrassing. Dad's fond of saying that when I came along, I hogged all the best genes and didn't leave enough for Eric to work with. On the rare occasion that she surfaces from her literary world long enough to notice, it really pisses Mom off when Dad says that.

Dad sits down across from me. He still looks annoyed, but he smiles at me. "At least I got one son who actually achieves. Do you know why your brother couldn't manage to remember the fire? He was too engrossed with some stupid present he's making." He drains his mug, scowling again. "Worthless." I'm not sure if he's muttering about the present or about my brother.

There's no point in saying too much when Dad gets going about Eric. Personally, I think he's a bit hard on the kid sometimes. But I suppose he's right. Eric's going to have to get it together someday. I think Dad's about given up on him as it is—it's been years since he's let Eric help us outside with anything. You have to know what you're doing for Dad to want to work with you.

"You boys have both had everything handed to you, but at least you've used those advantages to be successful. Your brother certainly hasn't done anything to deserve what he's been given." Dad thumps his empty mug onto the table and drops his spoon into it with a clatter.

"He wouldn't have lasted five seconds growing up the way I did."

Dad's very proud of the fact that he grew up poor and made himself into a six-figure earner with no help from anyone. "Those whiners who go around crying they can't win because they were dealt a shitty hand—they make me want to puke," he always says. "I came from nothing and look at me. You can rise above *anything,* as long as you have the balls to get up off your dead ass and do it."

Needless to say, Dad doesn't have much sympathy for low achievers.

"Enough breath wasted on that." Dad gets up and walks through the entryway to the stairs. I carry his mug and mine to the dishwasher and go into the living room, where the fire has mysteriously been resurrected and is crackling away.

"What're you making?" I ask. Eric's sitting on the floor by the coffee table, surrounded by a mess of tissue paper, ribbons, and other gift-wrapping fallout, and he's drawing something. He looks upset, like he always does after having it out with Dad. He never says too much, though.

"Wrapping paper." Eric sets down a black felt pen and picks up a red.

I plop down on the marble hearth to finish thawing out. "You know, Eric, most of the first world actually buys wrapping paper."

Eric laughs. "This is for Kristin—she's testing for her red belt next week." He brings the sheet of paper over and hands it to me. Eric's no Botticelli, so it's a bit tough to tell, but it looks like he's covered it with rows of little people in those white pajama-looking karate outfits. They're each punching and kicking in different ways, but they're all wearing red belts and have ponytails. I guess he was trying to draw Kristin.

"You're giving her poorly drawn wrapping paper?"

"Ha-ha." Eric takes a box off the coffee table. "It's going around this." He opens the box and takes out a silver necklace with a charm shaped like a four-leaf clover. "It's for good luck on her test."

My back's starting to roast, so I lie down on the Turkish rug to go back to medium-rare. "Wait a minute. You said she's taking this test or whatever next week?"

"Yeah."

"So you're going to all this trouble for this girl, and she hasn't even done anything yet? What if she fails her test? Then you've done all this shit for nothing."

Eric puts the silver clover back in the box and starts wrapping it with his little kicking-chick paper and some silver and red ribbons. "Well, then I've just done it for her, I guess." He picks up the tape. "That's not nothing."

I shrug. Eric's more than a little out there sometimes. He's probably just spent over an hour custom-wrapping this stupid necklace, to say nothing of the time and money it took to go out and get the thing in the first place. And for what? Because this girlfriend of his probably threw out some hints that she wanted him to get her a little something. I certainly don't put up with any crap like that, and I can't see why Eric would want to.

"A chick-whipped guy, little brother, is probably one of the most pitiful sights there is." I sit up and go back to the fire to roast myself again.

Eric looks up from his stupid curly ribbon. "Who's chick-whipped?"

"You see anyone else in this room?"

"So I'm whipped because I buy my girlfriend a present?"

"You're doing something that's unnecessary. You can't tell me you enjoyed hanging out in the freaking jewelry department looking at pretty little necklaces?" A log pops in the fire behind me, making me jump.

"That's not the point, Dane."

"I don't know what the hell is, then. It's not like it's Christmas or anything."

"Speaking of holidays, isn't Elise's birthday this week?" Eric sets his masterpiece on the coffee table. "Aren't you going to get her something?"

"I doubt it." I did get her something last year, but then we'd just started dating and were still in that stupid phase when we wanted to be together all the time and shit, so I guess it seemed like the thing to do. But we've been together over a year now, so I don't see the point.

Besides, she still hasn't called to apologize for her little performance at the party the other night.

Eric shakes his head. "I really don't get you sometimes."

"Mutual. Definitely mutual." It's true. I like the kid okay, don't mind talking to him once in a while, but more than once I've wondered how we ever ended up doing the doggie paddle in the same gene pool.

Or rather, he doggie-paddles and I butterfly.

Eric finishes gathering up the debris from his adventures in wrapping and walks out of the living room. The little ribboned box sits on the coffee table, a testimony to my brother's sad desire to please other people.

The heat from the fire is making me drowsy. I'm trying to decide whether to get started on an AP bio lab report that's coming due or just take a nap when Eric sticks his head back through the doorway.

"Someone's here—I think it's Jeff."

So much for productivity *or* slumber.

I haven't talked to Jeff since his party the night before last. To his credit, he did show up and put in a decent practice yesterday, in spite of what must have been a truly phenomenal hangover. But he took off like a man trying to outrun the hounds of hell about a nanosecond after we finished.

I go out onto the snow-covered front porch and amuse myself by throwing snowballs at Jeff as he picks his way up the icy sidewalk. He threatens to give me an up-close view of the inside of a snowbank, which is entirely in his power to do. At 6'1" and 180, I'm no shrinking violet by any standards—unless being compared with Jeff's truly huge frame.

I'm unimpressed by his threat—Jeff's too much of a teddy bear to do anything more than toss a few snowballs back my way—but I lay off my aerial onslaught and let him get to the porch. "You dug your way out of an ice storm just to partake of my company? Jeff, I'm touched."

Jeff doesn't answer. Up close now, his eyes are bloodshot and bruised-looking. He stops at the bottom of the steps, one hand on the railing. "I need to talk to you. Can you come for a drive?" He gestures to his ancient Saab, chugging and sputtering in the driveway.

"A drive? In this crap?" I look at the fishtail tracks in the snowy road that Jeff slid in on. "We can go talk in my room."

Jeff looks uneasy. "Is your family home?"

"Just Dad and Eric." Not even the second Ice Age could stop Mom and her SUV from her Sunday morning sessions at her office.

"What about Elise? Will she be around today?"

He looks even more worried as he says her name, which is mildly annoying.

But I let it slide. Jeff's puppy-dog crush on Elise isn't any threat to me. And anyway, in the eleven years Jeff and I have been friends, he hasn't done too many things to let me down. Our symbiosis has been mutually beneficial, all things considered, which is why I have a little more patience with him than with most other people.

"Elise won't be here," I tell him. "Come on, get your butt inside." I go into the house while he skids back down the sidewalk to turn off his car.

"What's on your mind?" I ask when we're in my room.

Jeff collapses into my red woven hammock that's strung across a corner from two metal rings. "The other night," he says, planting a foot on the wall to push himself back and forth.

I laugh and sit down on the bed so I can lean against the wall. "You were a star, that's for sure. Did McNeal show you the pictures?"

Jeff whips his head around to look at me, almost dumping himself out of the hammock. "*Pictures?*" he whispers, his voice strangled. "Oh, God."

"Don't worry. You could only see your ass in most of them. I think McNeal's planning to get one framed for you."

Jeff closes his eyes and rocks himself harder. "I'm such an asshole, Dane. I don't even remember doing those things with— *to*—Angie. Ash told me yesterday morning when he woke me up for practice."

"Did Angelica remember anything?"

"I don't think so. Not until someone told her."

"Ease up on the wall, huh? You trying to put a hole through it?"

"Sorry." Jeff opens his eyes and stops drilling the wall with his foot. He stares up at the ceiling. "This whole thing is just so messed up. I mean, how could I have done something like that? And why didn't anyone stop me?"

Guess he doesn't even remember Elise's attempt. I pull a pillow from behind my back and toss it at him. "Hey, don't sweat it. Sure, we all may have questioned your sanity for dating Angelica in the first place, but it wasn't any secret what the two of you do together. It's certainly not like she's any pure little princess."

Jeff's not looking any less depressed, so I search for a few more random lines to add to the pep talk. "So you'll take some crap at school for a few days, but it'll be old news before you know it. Embarrassment over. You'll be fine."

The hammock's stopped rocking completely. Jeff's staring at me oddly, almost like he doesn't recognize me.

"Dane, I wasn't talking about me being embarrassed. I meant what I did to *her.*"

FLORIDA

April 6, 10:59 a.m.

"All right, that's good for now. Why don't we call it a day?" Anya spins her wheeled stool around and reaches toward the control pad on the e-stim machine.

"No, leave it on." I can't turn my head to look at her as I say it, because I might fall over. I focus on my left leg, mentally ordering it to lift itself as high as the right one did a few seconds ago.

Anya punches a few buttons. The machine switches off and the current stops running through my leg, which crashes back to the mat.

"Turn it back on!"

"No."

I'm sitting on the edge of a low, mat-covered table in the PT/ OT gym. If it can accurately be called sitting, that is. In actuality, I'm leaning back on my arms, which Anya has arranged out at forty-five-degree angles behind me and braced against the mat. As long as my hands and shoulders stay precisely positioned, my elbows won't buckle and topple me backward. While I'm concentrating on keeping myself upright, I'm also working on making my legs move. Anya sticks little pads onto my skin and attaches them to this electricity machine with plastic-covered wires. I still can't contract the muscles in my legs enough to straighten them on my own, but I can when the electricity zaps them and gets them started for me. It feels crazy, like bugs dancing over my skin with electrified tap shoes.

But it works.

That is, until someone gets cute and decides to kill the energy source.

Anya turns away from the machine and wheels her stool back over to sit in front of me.

"Dane, you've done really well today. Better than I was expecting, to tell you the truth. But you have to rest, too. If you push it too hard, you're going to damage your muscles instead of making them stronger."

Yeah, whatever. "Come on, Anya, I wasn't finished. Just turn it back on for a minute." I know I can make that left leg work as well as the right one. "I'm not even tired yet."

Anya raises a red-blond eyebrow. "Oh, so you're just pouring sweat and sucking wind like a three-pack smoker out of sheer boredom, then?" she says. "You still think I'm that easy to put one over on?"

Not for the first time in the past hour, I have a profound urge to smack the smugness out of her. She must absolutely get off on being able to control almost every aspect of my physical activity. After she and Joel caught up to me with the golf cart the other day, Anya actually had the nerve to confiscate my wheelchair for two entire days.

And was it really necessary for her to point out that it takes everything I've got just to hold myself upright in a pitiful semblance of sitting for a few lousy minutes?

"I'm not trying to put one over on you. I just mistakenly thought that my physical therapist would be interested in helping me do as much as possible, instead of trying to hold me back."

Anya puts on her serious, I'm-the-therapist-and-I-know-best face. "Dane, you know that's ridiculous. And if you've been listening to me, you also know that you can't overdo things this early on. Your body can only repair itself so quickly, and we have to respect that and work with it accordingly."

Tell that to my father. I don't answer her.

Anya keeps going. "It's coming back, you know. Sure it's slow, but that's just the way it is. You have to have some patience. Right?" she says, looking at me for some sort of wide-eyed, grateful response to her sound bites of prepackaged wisdom.

Okay, enough already. "Pep talk over?" I ask, trying to slow my breathing down enough so that my voice sounds appropriately bored.

Anya rolls her eyes. "Yes, let's stop annoying each other for the day." She ditches her stool to get into the right position to help me from the mat back into my wheelchair. She crouches down in front of me with her back straight and her ass out and pinches my knees together between hers. Then she arranges my head and shoulders forward over one of her shoulders and gets her hands under my butt. She rocks herself backward and flips me up and over into the wheelchair in one smooth motion. I hate having to let her do that, but I also have to admit that Anya's a hell of a lot stronger than she looks.

When she first started slinging me around like that, I was sure she was going to drop me, but she never has. Joel does it that way, too, but she's as good at it as he is.

I can help a little with my arms now, but today I'm mad enough at her that I just let her do it all on her own. I even lean back a tiny bit to make it harder on her.

I leave the therapy room without saying good-bye. As I head down the hall, Anya sticks her head out the door and calls after me.

"Maybe you can get Joel to help you with a shower for OT today—you could sure use one!"

I'm sure he'd rather help you with one, princess. That's what I almost yell back at her. But I can't sell Joel out like that, even to put Anya in her place. Instead, I just ignore her and keep cruising up the hallway toward my unit.

I'm not in the best of moods today, and my latest session with Anya hasn't served to improve that. She keeps yapping at me to do this or that, but what does she really know about any of it? It's pretty damned easy to stand around and tell someone what to do when you've never been in their place. I've only got so much time to spend on this whole rehab thing before I need to get it together and get back to my real life.

But she doesn't seem to get that, with all her talk about taking it slow and listening to my body, and all that other crap she spouts off. All I know is I'm not making progress with Anya as fast as I am with Joel. In OT, I can already use my hands enough to hold things if they aren't too small, and I can tell that my arms are getting stronger, too. But here I am in PT, unable to even kick my legs out without help from an electricity machine and struggling like hell to even sit quasi-upright. Never mind standing.

And that has to mean that Anya's not doing as good a job as Joel is. And her not doing her job is affecting my ability to do mine as well as I should.

I did sweat a lot during PT today, and my clothes are sticking to me in wet, salty patches, but I have no intention of asking Joel to help me with a shower later on. It's bad enough that he, as my OT, is the one in charge of helping me relearn how to do the things that they call "activities of daily living" around here, which include all of the most intimate and embarrassing aspects of personal hygiene—getting dressed, taking a bath, taking a piss, you name it. It was enough of a nightmare having Letitia do those things for me when I couldn't do any of it myself. But now that I'm starting to be able to move my arms more, to have another guy—one who I actually consider a friend—reteaching me how to do them?

Excruciating.

Though I will say that Joel is pretty cool about it. I don't know why the hell he ever chose a profession with such a lousy job description. I'll have to remember to ask him about that sometime.

Anyway, I think I'll try to find Letitia and sweet-talk her into helping me get washed up and changed before OT. Then Joel and I can work on something else more interesting, and I won't be subjected to any more humiliation than absolutely necessary.

Letitia isn't at the nurses' desk when I get back to the unit. About half of the patient rooms are arranged in a circle around the desk and the others are down a short hallway. I wander a little and finally hear her voice booming from one of the rooms at the end of the hall. I decide to wait around by the desk until she finishes whatever she's doing in there and comes back.

But ten minutes later, Letitia hasn't emerged and I'm getting bored, so I head toward my room to see if I can manage to maneuver the new Florida wildlife book Joel just gave me from my bedside table onto my wheelchair tray. It'll probably take forever, but it'll give me something to work on while I'm waiting for Letitia, rather than sitting here like a doorstop. And if I do manage it, I want to see if I can figure out how to turn the pages by myself. I can't work it with my fingers just yet, but I think if I use my palm instead I might be able to do it.

As I reach my doorway, I notice that Robert's door is open, which usually means that his wife isn't there. I look inside and see that I'm right. Carissa isn't around, either, but that often means that she's just outside being angry somewhere. Her mom, though, is usually here for a pretty good chunk of every day.

I'm not sure exactly what it is that motivates me to go into Robert's tomb-still room. Generalized curiosity, perhaps, or maybe I just feel the need to be around someone who's in worse physical shape than I am. There aren't too many people who fit that description at the moment, even around this place.

He looks as creepy as ever, arms curled up, legs thrust stiffly straight, mouth still frozen wide open. Up close now, I can see the silver fillings in some of his molars. The skin around his gaping mouth looks stretched and cracked, his hair's lank and oily, and his whole face has a greasy gray quality to it that doesn't even seem human. A thick, blue tube runs from the whooshing machine on the table beside the bed to a plastic thing fitted into what looks like a hole in his throat.

Gross. I'm glad that I just had a tube down my throat when I couldn't breathe on my own, rather than having a hole punched directly through it.

Feeling strangely sneaky, almost like a burglar or something, I look around Robert's room and my attention's caught by a white bulletin board above his bed. Words are scrawled across it in red dry-erase marker. *Good morning, sweetie!* ☺ *Today is April 6. We went down to Fort Myers for the day to see Aunt Jeannie. We'll tell her you send your love. Work hard in therapy today, and we'll talk to you tonight! Miss you lots! All my love, always, Eva.*

I seriously doubt that Robert will be sending his love anywhere anytime soon. Sorry, Aunt Jeannie. And working hard in therapy? I'm not sure what Eva's been smoking, but it must be pretty hard-core.

All the same, I feel a little strange reading such an obviously personal message, even though the person who it's intended for sure isn't going to get anything out of it.

It's mildly embarrassing, like when you sit next to someone on a plane and they end up telling you their life story, even though you don't want them to.

I turn my attention to the rest of the room, which is as much of a still life as Robert is. Silver-framed pictures line the walls and the dresser, which also has a soot-stained, obviously used firefighter's hat resting on it. Faces smile out of the pictures. A bunch of guys in turnout gear standing in front of a fire truck. Eva in a blue dress, looking younger, happy, unwilted, holding the arm of a strong-looking guy with dark hair and moustache and a ruddy complexion. The same guy swinging a giggling little girl through the air, her light brown braids flying out behind her.

It takes me a full minute to realize that the guy has to be Robert. Is that little girl Carissa, then? I look closer at the picture.

Yes. Those ashy gray eyes are exactly the same.

There are other pictures of her. In one she looks about seven years old, posing in a green and white soccer uniform and holding a ball, her grin showing three missing teeth. Robert's (did Robert *really* ever look like that?) arm is around her.

It's like looking at a storybook, a window into some picture-perfect world out of some fantasy past that was buried under the crush of reality.

If it even existed in the first place, that is. There sure aren't many pictures like this lying around my house.

I look back, away from the past-life Robert of the pictures to the real-life Robert in the bed, and I jump.

His eyes are both wide open. And I'm dead sure they weren't when I came in less than two minutes ago.

Now I'm freaked out. When Robert's eyes were closed, it was easy to just think of him as an inanimate part of the room, another piece of furniture. But having his eyes wide and staring like that changes everything, even though he doesn't seem to be looking at me. Or at anything, for that matter.

Looking at his pictures, his notes, and the rest of his personal things, I suddenly feel like an intruder.

For a moment, I'm tempted to just turn around and make tracks to my own room. Letitia has to be almost finished with whatever she was doing anyway, and I don't want to have to explain what I'm doing in here if she walks past and sees me. Especially since I'm not even sure why I'm here.

But I don't leave. Instead, I drive my chair over to the side of Robert's bed. "Hey. How's it going?" Stupid question, but what else is there to say to someone you know absolutely nothing about?

Did his eyes flicker for a second when he heard my voice? No. I'm pretty sure they didn't.

It feels seriously weird to talk to someone who's about as responsive as a banana, but I try again. "I'm Dane. I have the room across the hall."

Silence.

I look once more at the cheery, unrealistic note about working hard in therapy on the dry-erase board above Robert's bed. "You're not really in therapy, are you? If you are, I hope you have the other PT. Mine's a pain in the ass."

Silence.

I'm running out of things to say to myself, so I think this is a pretty good time to leave. "Well, I guess I'll be going, okay? Maybe I'll stop back again sometime." I don't know why I would, but it seems like the right thing to say. I head toward the door and am almost out when something occurs to me. I stop and turn back around for a second. I look one last time at the Robert that is, the pictures of the family that was, and at that stupid, sad little message board.

"You know, you're not the only one who looks like a different person in those pictures," I say to the silence. "Your daughter sure seemed less angry when you were around."

It's not just the lack of anger that was different. Swinging through the air in her father's arms, holding the soccer ball with a gapped smile, Carissa looked truly happy.

Or the closest thing I've seen to it.

April 8, 1:07 p.m.

"Okay," Joel says, stretching out and making himself quite comfortable on my unmade bed. He folds his arms behind his head. "What's the surprise you've got for me?"

"Right. Here goes." I take a deep breath and concentrate on the closed book sitting on the tray table in front of me. My hand slides forward onto it, slowly but reasonably smoothly. My thumb hooks itself under a corner of the cover, then a sharp, rather awkward twist of my whole arm pulls it open. I repeat the whole process again. And again. And again.

It's taken hours of sweating and cursing my clumsy hands and accidentally knocking the book onto the floor and out of my reach. I must have rung the call bell about fifty times yesterday, but Letitia kept coming into my room and retrieving it for me every time without a complaint.

But it was worth it.

I can turn pages.

By myself.

The massive rush of triumph I feel is instantly dampened as I realize how crazy I am to feel all proud for accomplishing something that any two-year-old does without a second thought.

Suddenly, I'm embarrassed and annoyed with myself for acting like I had something meaningful to show Joel.

But my string of thoughts is interrupted by a loud whoop. I look up, startled, just in time to see Joel launch himself straight up and do a little victory dance right on my bed, trampling my pillow in the process. Then he leaps off onto the floor, almost landing on top of me.

"That's incredible!" he yells, pounding me on the shoulder. "How long have you been able to do it?"

"Just since yesterday. I probably spent six hours trying before I finally got it," I say, recalling the endless struggling and swearing before that first, ecstatic moment of success. "I guess it isn't really that big a deal, but I thought you might—"

Joel cuts me off midsentence. "Are you kidding? This is fantastic! I'm so proud of you!"

I think he means it.

After a bit, Joel gets me set up for today's task, which is shaving myself. He jacked up the handle of the razor with this thick foam-sleeve thing so I can get a better grip on it with my weak hands and hopefully avoid carving my face into hamburger in the process. After providing me with razor, mirror, and basin of hot, soapy water and dousing my face with shaving cream, he reinstalls himself on my bed to spectate while I struggle to get my face and the razor to match up as accurately and painlessly as possible.

"So they actually pay you to hang out in my bed?" I ask, concentrating on making contact with the skin on my right cheek without actually digging into it. While he does offer strategic suggestions and occasional words of encouragement, it seems that Joel's leaving me mostly on my own for today's fun-filled activity.

"Yeah. Beautiful, isn't it?" Joel stuffs another one of my pillows behind his head. "The better you get, the easier my job gets. Of course, I'm lending an invaluable supervisory role to the task."

"Right." I can't help laughing at that.

I work in silence for a few minutes, since I have to focus on what I'm doing. This is certainly a hell of a lot harder to do than it was six months ago, but it's also marginally easier than it was last week. And that has to count for something, right?

"Have you read any of this yet?" Joel picks up the Florida wildlife book that he gave me last week and thumbs idly through the pages. What wouldn't I give to be able to just flip through like that without even thinking about it?

"Uh-huh." I look up from the water-splashed and shaving-cream-spattered mirror for a second. "A lot of it." After I finally got the hang of turning pages yesterday, I probably stayed up half the night reading the book. Partly just because I finally *could,* but also because it's a damned-interesting book. "Especially the section on alligators."

"No kidding?" Joel looks at me over the pages of the book. "They're pretty interesting critters, aren't they?"

"Definitely. Especially their MO regarding the opposite sex."

According to the book Joel gave me, male alligators have a pretty smart approach to the whole courtship and mating thing. They each build their own pit out of dirt, which is essentially their home base. Exclusively so, for the majority of the time. They hang out alone in their respective pits until mating season comes along. Then they each choose a female, whom they'll invite into their pit for a brief period. After they take care of business, so to speak, they resume their former lifestyle, independent and unencumbered, until the next mating season rolls around. What a perfect way to do it. I think Thoreau would have approved, too. The ultimate method to eliminate the relationship-related bullshit that humans saddle themselves with.

Joel laughs. "It's interesting, but it definitely makes me grateful that I'm a person instead of an alligator. I mean, who'd want to have a companion for such a short time?"

"That's the great part about it, though," I say. "Just think about all the crap you wouldn't have to deal with that way."

"And just think about all that you'd miss out on that way," Joel counters.

I start to debate with Joel about this but stop myself, remembering how our last conversation about females ended up. I don't particularly want to get Joel mad at me again. I guess we're just going to have to agree to disagree on this particular topic. I focus my attention on my reflection in the mirror (my hair's getting long enough to seriously need tying back) and on removing the rest of the stubble from my face, which takes about half an hour but which I do completely on my own for the first time. And I manage it with only three minor flesh wounds, which is a huge improvement over my last attempt.

"Nice job," Joel says as he cleans up the debris from my personal-grooming adventure and splashes some stinging stuff onto the cuts I gave myself. "What do you want to do now?" he asks, tossing a towel at me. "My next patient's out on an appointment today, so we have some extra time if you feel like it."

"How about I take a nap?" I say, drying my face with the towel and clumsily mopping up the water that spilled on the wheelchair tray.

"Sorry. I already called dibs on your nap spot." Joel comes out of the bathroom, where he's ditched the water basin and razor and flops down on my bed yet again. "What's your second choice?"

I decide to do some arm exercises, which means Joel actually will end up having to haul himself out of my bed so we can go down to the therapy clinic and get some weights for me to use. But first, I want to change into some shorts. All the rooms inside this place are air-conditioned to the point of being absolutely glacial, so I generally wear long pants during the first part of the day. But it's starting to get downright hot outside, especially for a northerner like me, so I usually try and get someone to help me change into something cooler before I make my afternoon trip outside, which I'll do as soon as OT's finished.

"You know," Joel says as he undoes the button on my jeans and I use all the strength in my arms to push myself up against the wheelchair armrests so he can pull them off, "you're getting to the point where you could probably manage to get your pants on and off by yourself, don't you think?"

"Maybe." I'm not sure about that, though. I could probably pull them up or down, especially with the help of that long-handled stick with the claw thing on the end that Joel gave me to grip them with. But I doubt I'd be able to manage the zipper or the button without help—my fingers just can't contend with small things that require more fine-motor control.

Almost as though he's just read my thoughts, Joel continues, "I think it's the jeans that are holding you up. They're not at all stretchy, which makes them harder to get on, plus there's the button and stuff to deal with. What about wearing sweatpants, instead? Those would be the easiest to manage."

"Sweatpants? No way." Is he nuts? Who in their right mind
goes around in public wearing sweatpants?

Joel laughs. "Come on, Dane, it's not exactly a fashion show
around here, is it? It would make things a lot easier on you."

"Easy for you to say. You're not the one who'd have to go
around looking like a moron."

"You wouldn't look like a moron."

"Uh-huh. Right. Then why don't I ever see you and the rest of
your little band of thieves modeling that particular style?" Joel's
more the rugged, outdoorsy type, but Anya, Casey, and Thomas
(the other OT and PT) definitely dress on the preppy-casual side
of the spectrum.

Joel grins. "Letitia wears scrubs. You could look just like her."

"Very funny."

Joel's cracking himself up. "Okay, you want me to wear some?
I will. Just for you."

"I'll bet." I don't even know why I'm making such a big deal
out of this. Sure, wearing sweatpants probably would make it a
lot easier for me to be independent, at least as far as getting myself
dressed goes. And the rules of acceptable fashion are extremely
lenient here, encompassing everything from hospital gowns to
Isaac's plastic necklaces and glitter-caked hat, which rarely even
get a second glance from anyone.

Maybe it has something to do with Carissa's comment about
me looking like hell. Maybe it's the fact that the only other people
around here even remotely close to my age (other than a couple
nurses) are the therapists, who always look like regular, well-
dressed, good-looking twenty-something people.

And it's bad enough that I have to go around with a wheelchair, stuck in a body that only half works. I'm tired of looking acceptable by hospital patient standards. I just want to look like a noninstitutionalized eighteen-year-old again.

I want to look like myself.

Joel doesn't push the issue any further. Having gotten my bottom half stripped down to my boxers, he digs a pair of loose-fitting shorts from my drawer. He hands them to me, along with the clawed stick. "Here, see what you can do."

"All right." I drop the shorts onto the floor in front of me, then use the stick to grab onto them and work them over my feet and up my legs. As with just about everything else these days, progress is agonizingly slow, and seeing how pathetically shrunken my calves still are isn't much of a pick-me-up, either.

As I fight with the shorts, Joel leans against the closet and looks around my room. "You didn't bring much stuff here with you," he says, glancing over the bare walls. "Don't like clutter?"

"I wasn't in much of a position to decide one way or the other," I remind him, trying to make the shorts slide up over my knees instead of returning south to my ankles. It's tough to request that certain things come with you when you can't talk. I don't know what my parents did with the get-well cards and notes and pictures that were in my room at the hospital back in upstate. It was lucky that Eric thought to bring my iPod from home and stick it into one of my bags before I was sent down here. He even put some audio-books on there as a surprise. Other than that, though, there wasn't much in the way of personal effects that made the trip with me.

"Right. I forgot." Joel goes over to the dresser and studies the few things on top of it.

"I like this," he says, picking up the wooden loon from Elise that I never got around to throwing away, turning it over in his hands. "Who gave it to you?"

"I don't even remember," I say, thinking about Vermont last fall, lying beside Elise in a darkened tent and listening to the eerie shrieks and whistles of the loons echoing across Bourne Pond. Joel puts the loon back, beside the huge pine cone I scored off Carissa the other day. The only other thing on the dresser is a small pile of mail, mostly from Eric, who must get a kick out of finding the weirdest possible assortment of postcards to send me. In his first letter, he also sent a picture of himself in his karate uniform—I think his purple belt might be new, but I can't remember for sure—and one of my snapping turtle, possibly as proof that he hasn't yet killed him. There's also a short letter that Jeff sent last week.

Elise hasn't sent anything.

Joel picks up the postcards and pictures. "You want me to hang these up for you?"

"If you like." I've worked the shorts up to my thighs. Now I have to shift from side to side in the wheelchair to get them over my ass.

Joel slides the pictures into the frame of the wall mirror, studying each one in turn. "Your dad called Anya and me again yesterday to ask how your therapy's going," he says over his shoulder. "Did he tell you?"

Joel's a comedian.

April 8, 4:45 p.m.

"You need to be spending more time with Robert. How is he going to get better if he only gets one hour of therapy a day?"

Robert's door and mine are both wide open, so I have no trouble hearing the conversation that's shaping up between his wife and Anya. Or maybe *attack* is a better word, from the sounds of things. Eva isn't happy.

"Ms. Nielson, Casey and I are doing the very best we can for your husband. It's just more appropriate for PT and OT to see him together, since it takes two of us to do anything with him." Anya's voice sounds tired, like she's had a long day and this wasn't what she needed to finish it off. "Besides keeping his joints as mobile as possible so he won't get contractures, and putting him up on the tilt table to get some weight bearing for his bones, there's not really much else therapeutically that we can do for him at this point."

I risk a look out my door and across the hall. Through Robert's doorway I can see Eva in her usual stakeout spot beside Robert's bed, with her customary death grip on his stiff hand. Anya must be in one of the chairs on the other side of the room.

"Not much you can do? Is this not a rehabilitation facility? And are you not my husband's physical therapist?" Eva says, her voice tight. "He should be getting therapy for two hours a day, just like the rest of the people here."

"I can understand why you'd feel that way, but you have to realize that the patients who get two hours of treatment are in a little different situation than your husband."

"What is that supposed to mean, may I ask? My husband is a patient here as much as anyone."

"Of course he is, but his brain injury is also a lot more serious than most." Anya's voice is still calmly quiet and shows no signs of losing her temper. Which is surprising given the blatantly accusatory tone that Robert's wife is taking with her. "You do know that, don't you?"

Eva obviously isn't listening. "I don't care what you say. Robert needs more time in therapy, and you need to be working harder with him. If you were seeing him like you should be, he would be getting better. How will he be able to walk again if you don't strengthen his legs for him?"

I barely manage to conceal a snort of disbelief, then remember that I'm eavesdropping and pull my head back into my own room. Now I know Eva's not playing with a full deck. You don't have to be a therapist or a doctor to see that Robert's not going anywhere anytime soon. Does she actually believe what she's saying?

I don't know what she's expecting from Anya and Casey or where she gets the idea that they could be doing more for Robert than they already are. I've seen them in there together with him every day, doing serious manual labor over his frozen joints, hauling his twisted body on and off the tilt table, and talking to him as naturally as if he were hearing and responding to everything they said.

I hear Anya clear her throat. When she speaks, her voice is more gentle than I've ever heard it. "Ms. Nielson, admittedly, I haven't been working with your husband for very long, but I have done an extensive review of his medical history. His injury took place nearly four years ago, and as far as I can tell, there's nothing in his records to indicate that he's made any sort of functional progress in that time."

There's no reply. I'm pretending to read the open book on my tray table, but now I sneak another look around the door. Anya comes into view as she leans forward and reaches out to touch Robert's wife's hand. "Do you think it's at all possible," she says in that same uncharacteristically gentle voice, "that you're not being entirely realistic in your expectations of what we'll be able to do for your husb—"

Eva slaps Anya's hand away and cuts her off. "You're just like everyone else! All of you, always thinking the worst, never having any faith. You think you know everything; well, you don't. You don't know my husband."

"Ms. Nielson—"

"He's strong."

"I didn't mean—"

"He hears me. He smiled at me this morning."

Anya, seeming to recognize a lost cause, gives up on trying to get any more words in.

Eva plunges ahead blindly, a distinctly hysterical note threading through her voice. "He's going to wake up. He is! We'll show you; we'll show all of you!"

There's a sudden crashing noise from inside the room, as though someone just leaped out of a chair and slammed it back against the wall. For a split second I think it's Anya, but she hasn't moved. Neither has Robert's wife.

Then Carissa storms into view. I didn't even know she was in there. She stalks to the door, then spins back around for a second.

"Mom, shut the hell up!"

She whirls and strides out of Robert's room, slapping the door frame with her open hand as she goes through it. I quickly drop my eyes back to my book.

Just in time to suffer a near heart attack as Carissa bangs her way into my room, sending the door ricocheting off the wall so hard that it slams itself shut behind her.

"What did I do now?" I ask, even though I have an idea. From the look of flat-out rage on her face, I figure she saw me watching them again and is winding up to spew some venom my way.

But she doesn't. She throws herself onto my bed (why does everyone around here consider my bed free game whenever I'm not in it?), glares at the ceiling for a second, then rolls up onto her elbow and stares at me.

"I need someone at least marginally intelligent to unload on. You're going to have to do."

April 9, 2:02 a.m.

I wonder what it would take to bribe some sleeping pills off Letitia. I think I'm starting to need them.

I'm certainly no stranger to midnight ruminations, but I'm used to them being fueled by an upcoming Nordic race, a phenomenally expressed idea in a book, or an impromptu drive through the mountains to check out a lunar eclipse.

Now, crazily, it's people who are keeping me awake and tossing until the gray, predawn hours. Elise has been a major player, of course, which usually serves to irritate me. But Elise isn't the only one on my mind tonight.

I glance out the open door at Robert's room, which is dark and silent. Unless you'd been a witness, you'd hardly believe the drama that took place here this afternoon. Now it's like the room's completely deserted. I hook my arm in the bed railing and pull. I can finally get myself at least partway onto my side now, which means I can look out the window without giving my neck such an unpleasant workout. I always was a side sleeper, not that it's helping me get to sleep tonight. I'm still thinking back to this afternoon, when my bed was occupied by someone else.

When Carissa came crashing into my room, flung herself onto

my bed, and made her announcement that I was being drafted into service as her sounding board, the first thing that struck me was how quickly that girl can fill up a room. She has an overwhelming physical presence, a sense of restless, perpetual motion and barely contained energy that quickly expand to encompass the space around her. It reminded me, oddly, of Elise. With Elise, though, it's different. She can fill a room, too, but with her the presence is largely a mental one. Even when she's not saying anything, she radiates an enormous sense of subtly expressed intelligence. When Elise looks at someone, the thoughts ricochet behind her eyes almost visibly, and it's like she's able to see through to the person's very core.

With Carissa, on the other hand, all the ricocheting takes place with her constantly moving body, going so fast and so restlessly that you leave an encounter with her feeling like you've just played a Ping-Pong match in a hurricane.

"What's up?" I finally asked her when she didn't show any signs of being mad at me or of leaving. I wasn't exactly itching to talk to her after our last conversation, but even if I'd told her to take a hike, she probably wouldn't have. And anyway, I was pretty curious about what had just happened next door between Anya and Carissa's mom. "You seem even more in a twist than usual, so something must be wrong."

Surprisingly, she didn't even bite back at that, just rolled to her feet and closed the blinds on the windows between my room and the hallway. Then she came back to the bed, sitting down so hard the frame shook. She wrapped one of her braids around her neck and pretended to hang herself with it. "If this shit keeps up much longer, I'm going to do this to someone," she said, pointing to her hair-noose. "And it may not be to myself."

"Right, well," I said, "if you came over scouting out potential victims, I'm going to decline, thanks. I've got better things planned for my body than sacrificing it for your lousy temper. Why don't you try down the hall?"

Carissa threw a pillow at me. "Don't be a moron. I wasn't talking about you," she said, grabbing the pillow back and punching it a few times.

I looked at her more closely then and saw that her eyes were red, like she'd been rubbing them too hard. I was suddenly reminded of a little cat arching its back and hissing to look big, to act like it wasn't scared.

"Okay, then. Who were you talking about? You angry at your mom?" That seemed a logical guess, given the recent scene.

Carissa sighed explosively. "God, let's see. Who am I not pissed at these days?"

"I don't know. You tell me."

She paused, considering. "I guess it's more a question of what than who. And," she continued, "I'm pissed off because I've got no life and I'm fucking tired of it."

I wasn't impressed by this. After all, if the girl has no life, whose fault is that? "Is it really as tragic as all that?" I asked. "I mean, look at your dad—now he's got something to be upset over."

Before I even finished the sentence, Carissa was drilling a hole through my forehead with her ashy eyes. "Yeah, look at my dad, numbnuts," she snapped. "He's the lucky one in all this. He's on a free trip to perpetual la-la land—don't give me any shit about him being 'upset' over anything. He checked out a long time ago and left the rest of us to deal with the fallout."

I had to admit that she was right about Robert being checked out, but it still sounded sort of strange to hear someone talk like that about her own father.

"Okay, you're right. I shouldn't have said that. I'm sure it's got to be hard to have something like that happen to your dad," I said, realizing as I did that I still didn't know what happened to Robert in the first place.

She got up and paced around my room. "I'm over that. It happened four years ago—old news now. Only my mom has yet to figure out that little tidbit," she added. "And I'm the one who has to wait around in limbo for her to wake up and get a clue."

"Okay, so your mom's in denial about your dad. How does that put you in limbo?"

Carissa snorted. "Come on, New York. Who do you think gets dragged along for the ride every time my mom gets it into her delusional mind that the next hospital, the next rehab center's going to be the one to deliver the magic cure? I'm sixteen goddamned years old—do you think I enjoy living in shitty hotels, being home-schooled, and playing soccer with trees instead of on a team? You think that places like this," she said, gesturing at the hallway, "make for a really stellar place to spend your adolescence?"

I could definitely claim an informed opinion on the last question. "I'd imagine not. I've been here less than two months, and I've been ready to go schizo way more than once." A wild thought occurred to me. "Wait, you said your dad got hurt, what, four years ago?"

She nodded.

"And you and your mom have been doing this ever since?"

She nodded again. "Nice life, huh?"

Shit.

Carissa paced some more, winding up at my dresser. Like Joel did a few days earlier, she picked up the wooden loon. "This from your girlfriend?"

"Why would you think that?" I ask, a little defensively. I really need some other crap to put on my dresser to give people more variety when they want to paw my things.

"Just curious. I see you don't have any pictures of one up," she said, nodding toward the pictures of Eric and my turtle, "unless you like your women green, clawed, and carapaced. But who else would buy you a wooden bird, and why else would you bring it here with you unless it reminded you of someone you cared about?"

"Maybe I just like loons."

"Takes one to like one, I guess," Carissa said, setting the little bird back down. "But whatever. You can be secretive all you want; I don't really care."

"Who's secretive?"

Carissa didn't answer that, just flopped back onto my bed and leapfrogged to a new topic.

"So what's your real deal here, New York?" she asked, arching an eyebrow. "You're a pain in the ass, but at least you're breathing on your own and somewhat upright, so to speak. Are you stuck here for the long haul, or are you ever going to get out of this place? Head back north to your little Eskimo chick or whatever?"

"You bet your braided ass I'm getting out of here, and it won't be long, either. I'm already enrolled in summer school, and ski training won't be long after that." I didn't bother enlightening her about Elise. "What I have isn't a permanent thing."

"Yeah, that's what Anya said when I asked her about that disease you've got," Carissa said.

"You talk to Anya?"

"Of course I do. She's one of the therapists who isn't doing enough to miraculously cure my father, remember?" Her voice was a pretty accurate imitation of her mother's.

I thought about the way Robert's eyes opened when I was in his room. "So doesn't anybody know if your dad will get any better? I've heard your mom tell people that he opens his eyes and stuff."

Carissa snorted. "Right. And he always smiles at her right before someone comes into the room. But—surprise!—nobody else ever seems to see it. His eyes fall open for a second and she thinks he's waking up. He grunts and she's convinced he's whispering *I love you* to her. My mother's delusional, New York."

Carissa kicked her sneakers against the footboard of my bed and stared at the ceiling. "You'll eventually get better and get out of here. And I, who wasn't even broken to start with, will continue to rot in some lousy hospital or other. While my mother—who's basically forgotten that she even has a daughter—pursues her quest to turn herself into as much of a zombie as my dad is. And therefore, things are never going to change for us."

Then she stopped kicking and spoke very quietly. "Unless I do something about it."

She didn't say anything more about either of her parents after that, just talked about the soccer team she used to play on and asked me about New York and Elise and skiing until her mother left Robert's room and she could sneak in to grab her soccer ball and make herself scarce. I told her to mind her own business about Elise, but it actually felt good to be around someone my own age for the first time in about forever.

And, as unlikely as I would have imagined it, Carissa and I do have something in common. Playing soccer is as much a part of her as skiing is of me, and they're parts that neither of us is in touch with right now. But talking about it with Carissa renewed my determination to be back on my feet in time for next season.

When she finally did leave, I looked at the clock and saw that we'd talked for over an hour, which surprised me. The only other person with whom I'd ever had conversations that long was Elise. She and I could always talk the moon to both horizons in the same night.

But I guess it's like that when you're passionate about so many of the same things. Or thought you were.

UPSTATE NEW YORK

February 20, 5:58 a.m.

Thud. The snowball disintegrates against Elise's bedroom window. No answer. I walk around the corner of the house and toss a second one. This one splats onto the door of her tiny, wrought-iron balcony.

Still nothing.

Finally, I abandon stealth and let loose with a rapid-fire volley, plastering the window, door, and brickwork with white, and almost pasting Elise in the head when she yanks the balcony door open and steps out barefoot. And ducks, fortunately.

"I'm assuming you know what time it is." Her hands are tucked into the sleeves of her red fleece robe and she's wearing her glasses that make her look like a naughty librarian. Her voice is soft and only a few degrees cooler than the snowdrift I'm standing in.

"What, you were sleeping?" I give her my most charming smile. It's about six a.m., and the sun's barely starting to stitch a pink glow through the dark gray sky.

My Lady of the Balcony doesn't appear amused. "Keep it down, okay? You may not care about letting me sleep, but at least have the consideration to not wake up everyone else," she says, trying to keep her voice low and sound annoyed at the same time. "Why are you here, anyway?"

"Didn't have a choice. I tried your cell. You wouldn't answer."

"Did you look at the clock before you called?"

"Yes, but I couldn't stand to be apart from you a second longer."

"Besides being an absolute crock, that's not nearly enough incentive to keep me standing out here freezing. See you later," she says, turning for the door.

What, does she think I'm standing around in the snow for kicks? "You're not heartless enough to leave me out here, are you? Won't you feel awful when the temperature drops and you have to see my pathetic frozen body whenever you look out your window?" I pretend to collapse into the snowbank. "See, it's happening already!"

Elise comes back onto the balcony, shivering. "Maybe you deserve it," she says, but she doesn't sound quite as pissed.

I throw myself down onto one knee and shake clasped hands up at her. "Oh, fair Lady Elise, your humble servant doth abjectly beg admittance to your dwelling!" Elise is a sucker for that Shakespeare talk.

"Dane, you wake up the kids and it's your funeral." Elise is trying not to smile.

"I beseech you to take pity on this poor sojourner who pines but for a closer glimpse of your radiant face!" I close my eyes and clutch my heart. "Your eyes! They are like ... cesspools!"

"Thanks a lot."

"Your skin! It is like ... mayonnaise!"

"Will you keep it down?"

I don't. "Your hair! It is like ... wet spaghetti!"

A snowball grazes my shoulder. I open my eyes and duck as Elise fires another one.

"All right, enough. I'll let you in, but only to make you shut up." She disappears into her room and I jog around the house so she can let me in.

The rest of the household wasn't awakened by my theatrics, so we keep our voices low as we drink hot chocolate in the kitchen and I tell her why I've come calling in the wee morning hours.

"You want to drive to Walden Pond?" she asks, her eyebrows arching almost to her bandanna. "Today?"

"Definitely. I've already got my stuff in the Jeep. We can leave as soon as you get yours together." I talk fast, heading off any possible objections that I've already anticipated. The trip out will take about six hours, give or take, so we can switch off the driving to finish up any last-minute homework before we even arrive. We'll get to Concord by around one and have a good three hours of daylight to explore Thoreau's hideaway, plus the chance to see the pond at night. The Weather.com report for Concord looks clear, so we should see some great constellations tonight. If we leave Massachusetts by ten at night, we'll take turns driving again and have no trouble pulling in for school by eight a.m., as long as we don't cream a deer or a moose somewhere along the way. As far as parental consent goes, mine already think I'm spending the rest of the weekend at Jeff's. Elise lives with her older sister's family, so she can pretty much come and go as she pleases.

I finish spilling the plan in one big breath and wait for her reaction.

Elise doesn't say anything for a minute, makes herself busy heating up some cinnamon rolls.

"What's the deal, Lise?" I can tell by her face that she thinks it's a great idea. Elise is always up for an impromptu adventure— that's one of the things I've always really liked about her. But she's not acting excited like she should be.

"Nothing," she says, retrieving the hot rolls from the micro- wave and plopping them onto the table in front of us. "It sounds like a great idea. I know you've been wanting to take a Thoreau pilgrimage for a while now."

"But …?" I know there's a big *but* lurking around here some- where. What's to think about? She should be halfway packed by now.

Elise unwinds her cinnamon roll into a long, sugary snake as she talks. "You're acting like everything's just fine now. What about the other night?"

"What do you mean?"

"Dane, it's been a week since Jeff's party, and we've barely talked to each other at all, let alone about what happened. Not to mention the fact that you blew off my birthday, too."

"This trip can be your birthday present, if you have to have one."

"I don't need a consolation gift, thanks, and my birthday's not even the bigger issue here."

Here it comes. I make the trip over here to invite her out for a great day, and she wants to fight about something that happened a week ago. I drink the rest of my cocoa silently.

Elise doesn't let it drop. "I mean, that whole thing was pretty serious, wouldn't you say? I did end up walking home alone after midnight. Were you even a little worried about me?"

"I figured you wouldn't have taken off if you thought you couldn't handle it. Besides, you took your snowshoes." I noticed they were gone when I left the party myself. "I bet it didn't even take you an hour to get back."

She shakes her head. "That's not even the real point, Dane. Me walking home was just part of all the rest of it."

I shove my chair back and take my dishes to the sink. "Look, Elise, if you want to fight, I may as well go by myself."

"Don't you get it?" She stands up, too. "I don't want to fight with you—I want to talk about something that's important to me. I want you to understand."

"Well, it seems like you're picking a fight to me." Shit. Why can't she ever just let something drop?

"Not wanting to ignore a problem isn't the same thing as wanting to fight about it." Elise starts to say something else, but doesn't. "Never mind, okay? I don't want to get into an argument."

And I don't feel like spending the day alone, *or* with someone who's in a snit. I lean back against the counter and look at her. "Look, the thing at Jeff's is over. Okay, maybe I shouldn't have let you go home alone. Do you want me to say *sorry* for that? Will that make you happy?"

Elise shakes her head, I'm not sure in response to which question. She doesn't say anything. I check my watch. Almost 6:15. I want to get on the road.

"The way I see it, we can do things two ways, Elise. We can choose to get hung up on and argue about things that have already happened. Or we can go out and enjoy a beautiful day. I'm offering you an opportunity that I think you'd be foolish to pass up. What do you say?"

Elise stands at the sink, bites her lip like she's thinking. I tug on a piece of her hair. "I'd love to have a day worth remembering," I tell her.

She turns around then, looks at me, and I know she's convinced. In ten minutes she's dressed, packed and ready.

We go.

We have an amazing time.

"God, what would Thoreau think if he knew you could now buy hot dogs and coffee within spitting distance of his beloved pond?" Elise drums her fingers on the steering wheel and shakes her head. "Why is it that the American Way seems to cheapen everything it touches into some kind of theme-park parody?"

It's after midnight now, and we're rolling west on Route 90 with the windows down and the heater cranked. The jazz CD spins itself out, the last track fading into silence, and I replace it with an old Bob Dylan–Johnny Cash duet.

"I don't think he would have been surprised," I say. Walden Pond itself was tourist-ridden and sanitized, but we passed up the fractured quotes inscribed on stones and the signs herding people around the pond and cut through the woods on our own. We managed to find a nearby pond that was completely deserted, still well within Thoreau's stomping grounds but virtually undiscovered by the tourist hordes that were perfectly, idiotically content to follow one another and the signs around and around Walden Pond on the human equivalent of a hamster wheel.

We stop at an all-night diner somewhere outside Albany for terrible coffee and kick-ass pie, swapping bites of blackberry for strawberry rhubarb and laughing over someone else's lipstick prints that never completely faded off the thick, white mugs.

Then it's back on the road, switching drivers and picking up the Adirondack Northway that'll take us most of the way home. Traffic's much lighter here, but there're more deer to watch for.

Elise falls asleep right before we cross into Adirondack Park, just north of the Saratoga Springs exit, curling like a caterpillar under the red-checked and evergreen-printed fleece blanket she gave me last Christmas. The silent highway unrolls ahead, silver ribbon in the moonlight, winding past frozen fields with mist hanging heavy over them.

The clock flashes 4:27 a.m. in icy blue digits. Another hour or two and I should be looking at a fantastic winter sunrise. The CD spins out, and I fumble one-handed for another one. I'm starting to nod off, so I look for something loud to keep me awake. But then I look over at Elise sleeping against the door and, for some reason that I don't quite understand, I slide in a mellow Mozart album instead. I'll charge up on some convenience-store coffee when I stop for gas in Schroon Lake.

Elise stretches in her sleep, sliding her wool-socked feet across the seat to rest against my thigh, startling me. Moonlight hits her face through the dark waves of her hair, making her look like she's dreaming secrets. I look away from the road to watch her for a second, and this Robert Frost poem I learned a million years ago comes and parks in my head:

I'm going out to clean the pasture spring;
I'll only stop to rake the leaves away
(And wait to watch the clear water, I may:)
I sha'n't be gone long.—You come too.

I'm going out to fetch the little calf
That's standing by the mother. It's so young,
It totters when she licks it with her tongue.
I sha'n't be gone long.—You come too.

You come, too.

I guess that really sums up the way I feel about Elise sometimes. Frost talks about pastures and calves and watching water, and that's exactly it, those are the times. On a fall morning when the air's just starting to bite and the apple orchard's open. When I discover a new lake to take the canoe out on, or when the Jeep's gassed up and the road atlas is opened to a brand-new destination page.

Those are the times when something in me just calls for Elise to come, too.

FLORIDA

April 9 , 2:49 a.m.

See what happens when you let your thoughts get away from you?
This is exactly the kind of stupid thinking that makes people even
more stupid.

Thoreau and the alligators had it right from the start.

I don't need people. I need a pit.

April 9 , 7:55 a.m.

The sun's already hot and turning the early morning fog into a steamy haze that hangs over the wide lawn in front of the main building. I'm parked beside one of the pillars on the huge front porch, using Joel's binoculars to watch a green heron that's perched in one of the palm trees in front of me.

I'm pretty whipped, having accomplished almost no productive sleeping whatsoever last night. I finally gave up, stopped tossing, and convinced Letitia to help me get dressed and into my wheelchair as soon as it was remotely light outside. I've been out and about for almost an hour now, catching all the early morning activity in the pond and the woods that you usually miss once the day gets fully started.

Elise and I used to do this together back in New York. We'd take my canoe out while mist was still rising from the lake in frigid curls and the sun hadn't yet broken over the horizon.

A sharp whack on my right arm almost makes me drop the binoculars and abruptly reminds me how drastically my company for this activity has changed since those days.

"Hey, watch it."

I'm sharing the porch with none other than sparkly Isaac, who

I'm not at all convinced is supposed to be wandering around out here unsupervised. After trying to avoid him for a while, I finally gave up and let him join me. He's actually not that bad. He doesn't talk any more than Robert does, but at least that means he doesn't scare away any of the birds and animals that I'm trying to watch, and he even seems to take an interest in them himself.

Since he doesn't talk, though, he gets my attention whenever he notices something that he finds interesting by giving me his powerhouse version of a subtle tap on the arm, which invariably nearly knocks me out of my chair. In the end, I'm the one who's more likely to scare things away with a surprised exclamation.

"You've got to tone that down, man," I say, regaining my precarious grip on the binoculars. I follow Isaac's pointing finger to the ground beneath a thicket of yellow-flowered shrubs halfway across the lawn, where a ring-necked pheasant is lying almost motionless in the grass. I wouldn't even have seen it.

"Nice one," I say appreciatively. "You want to check it out?" Isaac nods, and I hand him the binoculars, though I do keep the strap looped around my forearm. They're not mine, after all, and there's no telling what use Isaac could conceive for them.

He watches for a few minutes until the pheasant flies away, startled by the noise of a car approaching on what has to be the world's longest, curviest driveway. You can't even see the road from here, and Joel's told me that it's almost a half mile from the main building. Isaac carefully sets the binoculars onto my wheelchair tray as a green Outback emerges through the banyan trees. Looks like it's Joel's turn to drive. This place is so far out in the sticks that the therapists generally carpool in together, since they all live about forty-five minutes away over on the coast.

For no particular reason, I watch through the binoculars as Joel pulls into the staff parking lot. He kills the engine and they all pile out. Anya stretches and yawns, rubbing her eyes, while Joel valiantly tries to ignore the way her arched back thrusts her breasts forward against her blue shirt. Casey's juggling a travel mug and doughnut while running a comb through her short blond hair. Thomas dives into the backseat to retrieve a forgotten stack of papers.

They've only taken a few steps toward the building when I notice that something looks really weird about them. From the waist up, they're all dressed in their normal clothes, but their bottom halves are a completely different story.

They're all wearing sweatpants. Crazy ones.

Casey's are peppermint-striped and huge, Thomas's are red and covered with gaudy Christmas lights. Anya's got a strange black and purple tie-dye, and Joel's are printed with the characters from *Green Eggs and Ham*.

I can't help laughing as I watch them approach the porch, Casey tripping over her too-long pant legs and almost sending her mug flying into a bird-of-paradise plant. They climb the steps, completely straight-faced, to where Isaac and I are sitting.

"Morning." Joel reaches into his messenger bag and pulls out something wrapped in a brown paper sack. "Here's something for OT today, Dane. See you then?" He deposits the bag on my lap, and he and the rest of the crew head through the sliding doors and into the building. Isaac, apparently tiring of my company, trails after them.

I slowly work the bag open, look inside, and laugh again. It's another pair of ugly sweatpants. These are bright green and have "I ♥ NY" printed all over them.

I guess I'm going to have to let Joel win this one.

That was nice of him—of all of them, actually. Although I suppose they're only doing it to make me do their bidding.

But it still feels sort of good.

April 19, 2:00 p.m.

I lean over as far as I can and inch my fingers along the mat. They just manage to close around the last beanbag. Then I pull myself back, lifting my torso until I'm sitting on the edge of the mat table like I started out. I fire the beanbag to the other side of the therapy room, where Anya and Joel are spread out on the floor with an assortment of tools and wheelchair parts. Above their heads, the window I convinced them to open (why waste a great breeze on an unusually mild day?) lets in the smell of flowers and freshly mown grass.

The beanbag bounces off the back of Joel's head. He jumps, dropping his socket wrench. Anya, who surreptitiously watched my entire windup and delivery with a professional eye over Joel's shoulder, nods approvingly. "Good eccentric biceps control there."

"Nice one." Joel rubs his head where the missile landed, then picks up the beanbag and lobs it back to me. "You're getting some power back in those arms. Now finish up what we asked you to do, okay?"

"I did."

"Really?" Joel says, surprised. He gets up and crosses the room, where he sees that I've retrieved all the colored beanbags he scattered around and behind me on the mat and tossed them all into the bucket standing halfway across the room. Okay, all but three that didn't quite make it in.

"Well done!" Joel retrieves the three escapees and tosses them into the bucket, which he stashes under the mat table. "Is that getting too easy for you?"

"It's starting to." Finally. It's taken a freaking long time for me to regain enough muscle control in my trunk and arms to coordinate the deceptively simple-looking chain of motions for that task. But I've finally got it, and well enough to do it in a reasonable amount of time.

PT and OT are combined today. Joel and Anya do that sometimes when they want to join forces and brainpower to work on certain things with me. It's kind of fun that way. Joel slips into comic-relief mode in order to keep Anya and I from bashing heads too much, which makes things more productive all around. I also get a kick out of watching Joel try and play it cool around Anya, who seems to like him just fine but doesn't appear to be aware of his unspoken worship. She never engages in any sort of flirting with him, casual or otherwise.

Not that Joel has the guts to flirt with her in the first place, of course.

"Okay, then," Joel says. "Let's try something a little harder. Close your eyes." I give him a suspicious look but do as he asks. With my eyes shut, it's already a little more difficult to keep myself sitting upright, but Joel stops me when I reach down to the mat I'm sitting on for support. "No. Keep your arms up."

I crack one eye. "Why?"

"Trust me. Just do it."

"If you say so." I close both eyes again and feel a gentle push against my chest. I'm not ready for it and almost lose my balance.

My eyes fly open. "What the hell?"

From across the room, Anya looks up from her repair work. "Weak, Joel. You've got to shove him harder than that."

Joel sneezes, then laughs, I think at both of us. "This is a really good way to work on your balance, Dane. Honest. If you don't expect where the push is coming from, your body has to work a lot harder to stay upright."

"So you're trying to knock me over?"

"Not if you can stop me. Now come on—try it again."

I don't know how these guys have gotten me to do so many weird-ass things like this. I half-suspect that they lie awake nights, thinking of crazy stuff to torture me with for their own deranged amusement. But I close my eyes again. "If you must."

Joel starts out gently again, then the pushes gradually start to come harder and faster, on my chest, my back, both sides. My abdominal and paraspinal muscles (I've been getting quite the anatomy education in therapy) quickly start to burn as they meet the strain of keeping me upright against Joel's randomly directed shoves, but they don't give out on me. I stay sitting up.

When Joel finally eases off, I'm sweating and my trunk muscles are more than mildly perturbed. But I did it.

"Awesome! Okay, take a rest," Joel says, which I'm more than happy to do. I reach down and grab hold of the legs of my sweatpants (yeah, okay, so I did end up agreeing to wear the stupid things), then hoist my legs onto the mat so I can stretch out comfortably. Joel flips a pillow under my head as I lie down, then Anya calls him over to hold a wheelchair frame for her while she hammers loose a stuck part.

I watch them work together for a minute. I have to admit they're a good team. Joel especially makes this whole rehab process as tolerable as possible. And Anya and I are even coming to endure each other marginally better. We still don't see eye to eye on much of anything, and I'm still not impressed by Joel's rationalization of her in-your-face personality as a blameless by-product of a so-called abusive relationship, but she does give me credit when it's due, and I, in all fairness, have to do the same.

As long as we don't try to agree on anything other than therapy, we manage to keep the symbiosis reasonably calm and fairly productive. I think Darwin would be proud of our adaptability.

I close my eyes and zone for a few seconds, concentrating on the beautiful sensation of my fingers opening and closing precisely when and how my brain tells them to. My top half has really started to take off in the past week. I can get myself dressed, brush my teeth, and my arms are strong enough for me to pull myself from the bed to my wheelchair with the help of a short wooden board that I use to bridge the gap. That alone has made a huge difference in my independence, since I can now come and go pretty much as I please without having to wait around for someone to have the time or the inclination to help me.

Joel comes back and sits next to me, sneezes again, and watches for a second as I try to make my legs move across the mat in all the different ways they're supposed to be able to. Anya's done it with them so many times that I know the routine cold ... slide out to the side like I'm making a snow angel ... pump ankles back and forth … bend my knees and try to make my foot touch my butt … tighten my quads enough to make my heels lift off the mat …

Thanks to Anya's almost brutal daily stretching, my legs aren't tight like they were when I first came, and she can move them through a normal full range of motion (it hardly even hurts when she does it now). But I still can't make them move like that by myself.

Which scares the hell out of me.

Joel sees me struggling to complete the right-sided snow angel and slides his hand under my calf to give me a little boost.

"Don't worry," he says. "You'll get it."

"Sure," I say, trying to sound completely unconcerned. But that's easy for Joel to say so casually.

He's not the one whose family is coming to visit in a week and a half.

I know—it was a complete surprise to me, too. I actually heard the news in a letter from Eric first, since he was really excited about the prospect of his first-ever trip to Florida. Then I got the rest of the details from Mom during her once-weekly, five-minute phone call. Since she's on sabbatical and Dad's only teaching one class and lab this semester, they decided to make the trek down here over Eric's vacation from school. They won't spend the whole time here, of course—probably just squeeze in a day or so between beach and museum visits to see exactly how well and how quickly I'm progressing with rehab.

Ten days until they arrive. That's not a lot of time.

And I'm still not even close to walking yet.

Sure, I blamed that on Anya at first. After all, my arms got moving and got stronger a whole lot quicker than my legs, which made it easy to assume that Anya wasn't doing her job for me. But I got hold of a textbook on neurological disorders and rehabilitation out of the therapists' office a few days ago and did a little research of my own. According to that, there's really no telling which muscles are going to come back exactly when, or even if they'll all come back fully.

Of course, there's absolutely no way I'll even consider the possibility of not making a complete bounce-back from this GBS stupidity. Seventy-five percent full recovery rate, remember? But I have had to admit that it may take a little longer than I originally anticipated.

And I have to at least be on my feet again by the time they arrive.

I turn my attention back to making my legs move and notice that Joel's no longer helping me along. I start to make a crack about him sleeping on the job, then see that something's seriously wrong.

Joel's hunched over on the table beside me, his shoulders rising and falling quickly. Too quickly. He's not making any noise, but his face is sweaty, grayish, and there's a weird bluish tinge around his lips. I sit up faster than I thought remotely possible.

"Joel? Joel, what's wrong?"

He shakes his head back and forth a couple times but can't seem to say anything. His mouth opens like he's trying to suck air, and I hear an awful, choking wheeze in his throat. I don't know what's wrong, don't know how to help him. Finally, I yell for Anya.

She's up and across the room in about a second. She kneels in front of Joel, gripping his upper arms. "You don't have it with you?"

Joel shakes his head, gasping.

"Is it in your desk?"

He nods.

"Okay, hold on. Dane, stay with him," she yells over her shoulder as she sprints for the door, as if I'd be going anywhere.

That awful, strangled wheezing fills the room. Joel's eyes are starting to roll, his hands vaguely scrabbling at nothing. Not knowing what else to do, I reach out and take hold of both of them. There's a creepy, sick feeling blossoming in the pit of my stomach as I stare at the dead blueberry-colored skin around his mouth.

"It's okay. It's okay." The words sound ridiculous, empty. "She'll be back; she'll help you." God, I hope she will.

After what feels like an hour but is probably only about fifteen seconds, Anya bursts back into the room at a dead run, something clenched in her left fist. It's an inhaler. She holds Joel's head upright with one hand while the other pushes the inhaler past his lips and shoves down the button to release the spray into his throat.

Almost immediately, Joel's wheezing turns back into breathing. It's shallow and painful-sounding, but it seems reasonably regular. He tugs his hands free from mine, drops his head into them, and sucks air like a pearl diver for several long minutes. Afraid that he might be passing out or something, I glance over at Anya, but she's just watching Joel, a frown—concerned, but not by any means frantic—creasing her forehead. She gets a washcloth from the linen shelf, wets it, and runs it over Joel's half-hidden face and hands.

"Just breathe, Joel. That's it," she says softly. "You're fine. You're going to be fine."

Finally, it's all over and Joel lifts his head. His face is still damp but no longer gray and blue, and his eyes have come back into focus, thank God.

"That was exciting." He smiles as he says it, but not terribly convincingly. He takes a few more breaths. "Thanks, An," he says, looking at the inhaler lying on the mat beside him. "I owe you one."

Anya's been pacing back and forth. Now she stops in front of Joel and me, arms crossed. She glares at Joel. "You can say that again. In fact, you owe me a heck of a lot more than that for the years you just took off my life. Will someone," she says, gazing toward the ceiling as if the answer might be caught in a corner cobweb, "please explain to me what might possess someone with incredibly bad asthma to decide that he doesn't need to keep his inhaler with him?" She looks at me like I should have the right response.

That was an asthma attack? Jesus, I had no idea they could be that bad—that was downright scary. I also didn't know Joel had asthma in the first place.

"I know, I'm an idiot …," Joel starts.

"Damned right." Anya's pacing again.

"Anya, I forgot. It happens sometimes. I'm just really glad you were here," Joel says. His voice is almost back to normal. "At least I actually had it in the building this time, right?"

Anya flops down onto the table, on Joel's other side, with a thud. When she speaks, her voice still sounds angry, but not only that. "Don't scare me like that again," she says quietly, looking hard at him.

"I won't. Promise." Joel leans back on his hands, then seems to remember that I'm still there watching. "You okay, Dane? You look like a ghost just walked in front of you."

"I thought one was going to for a minute there. You sure you're all right?" That's one scene I have no desire to relive.

"I'm good. They're usually not quite that bad, especially if I have my inhaler close at hand. I know it looks freaky when it happens, but I'm okay. Really," he adds when I don't look convinced. "Actually, you should be glad, since I just used up the last five minutes of your therapy session."

After I get back into my wheelchair (I'm now using one that I power with my arms), Joel walks out of the therapy room with me. "Sorry if I gave you a scare," he says. "Thanks for your help, though."

"Sure," I say, even though I can't see that I did a damned thing besides sit there, absolutely useless.

As I head through the sliding doors to the outdoors, I cross paths with Carissa, who's coming up the concrete ramp. She says hi, to which I barely answer.

"What's your problem, asshole?"

"Get lost." I go down the ramp without looking back. I'll talk to her later.

What's my problem? Good question. I'm worried about Joel, but it isn't just that. I'm also a lot more nervous about my family coming than I'm willing to admit.

I hit the path and start pushing myself in the direction of the gazebo that sits halfway around the pond. I push hard, making my arms tired almost immediately, but even that's not enough to distract me.

The last time my father and I talked face to face was the day of my first major screwup.

UPSTATE NEW YORK

February 22, 10:10 p.m.

"Dane?" Eric's voice is muffled through the door. Not enough, unfortunately. I sit up and crank the music high enough to drown out his voice. Then I throw myself back onto my bed and resume staring at the ceiling.

He knocks again.

"Hey, Dane," he shouts, barely audible under the music. "Don't listen to Dad, okay? You know he's just a hard-ass sometimes."

I study the framed prints on my wall. Maybe I should re-arrange them, maybe switch the aurora borealis with the Pacific loons.

Eric doesn't take the not-so-subtle hint. "Anyway, he probably didn't mean it—you're the star of this family, right? He'll get over it."

If I took down that old Escher print that's been up there for-ever, there'd be room to tack up the new constellation chart I just got, right next to the leaf sketch Elise made for my birthday.

"Come on. Let me in. You want to talk about it or anything?"

"No. Get lost."

Silence. But I know he's still out there. Eric's never been good at handling civil unrest in the House of Rafferty—never learned to let it just roll off like I have.

Finally I grab a book from beside the bed and bounce it off the door. "Get the hell out of here!"

The book didn't hit nearly as hard as it should have. I slap my hands against my thighs, trying to get rid of the strange tingly-weak feeling, trying not to think about it.

Minutes pass, then I barely hear his footsteps padding back down the hallway. Finally.

I run both hands through my hair, squeezing my temples. My damn head is killing me, and having the music at max decibels isn't helping.

I get up and pace around the room, trying to find something that I haven't yet tried and failed to refocus my mind on. I've already categorized my books, alphabetized my CDs, kicked my dirty clothes into the closet, and sacrificed four feeder fish to the baby snapper I snagged from the lake last summer and now keep in a tank on my computer desk.

The book I tossed was a leather-bound Steinbeck, which was a lousy choice to take my frustrations out on. Retrieving it from the floor, I see some pages got bent when it landed open. Shit. I unfold them one at a time and close the green cover over them, then take the book to my desk to squash under my heaviest field guide, a Sibley's ornithology. Hopefully a few days under the weight will make the pages lie flat again.

The little turtle is still tearing up chunks of the last fish, sinking in with his hooked beak and claws, shaking his head to rip each piece loose, then gulping it down. He eyes me suspiciously as I sit in my desk chair and lunges at the finger I tap against his tank.

Mom wasn't exactly thrilled when I came home with a baby snapping turtle and installed him in my bedroom, but she got

used to the idea. Now she thinks he's some sort of family pet—
whenever we have steak or chicken she always saves little pieces
for him. She also thought he needed a name, which I hadn't pro-
vided, so she calls him S.T. (short for *Sir Thomas*, she claims). I
suggested that she go ahead and tack on a *D* while she's at it, but
she just called me uncouth.

Me, I think naming animals is stupid as hell. Why do people
have this weird desire to turn animals into something other than
what they are, to give them dumb people names and teach them
dumb people tricks, instead of actually paying attention to the
things that animals already do on their own?

"He thinks he's a person." How many times have I heard that
anthropomorphic crap from some idiot describing their dog or
their cat or their freaking gerbil? If you want a little person, why
not go to the orphanage and get yourself a stray kid?

That's why my turtle doesn't have a name.

After that huge snapping monster almost chomped me last
summer, I got interested in these critters. Not wanting to tangle
with another three-footer, I decided to catch a little guy instead
and ended up netting this one. He's only about four inches across
the carapace, no more than a couple years old at the most, but
he's already aggressive as hell. Even though I'm the food, clean
water, and UV-light provider, making me the supreme deity of
his little shelled existence, he'll still try and take a bite out of me
whenever he gets the chance.

Sure, he paddles over to the side of the tank and waits expec-
tantly when he sees me approaching with food. But I'm not stupid
enough to mistake that for affection on his part.

And that's okay. He is what he is. Our relationship is the

perfect symbiosis. He gets all his necessities taken care of, plus extra choice tidbits from Mom, and I get to observe him up close whenever I want.

Liking me doesn't have to be a part of the deal, and it shouldn't be, either. We each get what we want out of the arrangement.

I rest my forehead against the tank. The cool glass feels good on my pounding head. I stare down at the turtle, who stares back at me with his prehistoric face, a shred of fish skin and fin dangling from his jaws. My cell phone rings and I jump, knocking my head on the glass.

"Shit!" The turtle scrambles for the other side of the tank as I rub the new sore spot on my forehead with one hand and reach for the phone with the other. I pick it up and look at the name blinking on the screen: JEFF.

Nope. Forget it. Ten to one he's calling to talk about today's race, and I'll be damned if I'm going to talk about that with anyone. Or even think about it. I let the phone ring until the voice mail picks up, then turn it off and drop it in the trash can.

There.

I'm not fooling myself, though.

I'm still thinking about it. And as hard as I've been trying to convince myself otherwise, I can't think about anything else.

I tap my fingers against the glass again, and a tiny jolt of electricity shoots up into my hand with each tap. My feet haven't fully stopped tingling since this afternoon, either.

This shit's getting weird.

Just like what happened to me during the race today. I bite my lip as I think about how I blew it this afternoon.

How I fucked up.

I don't even know what exactly went wrong. The race started out straight-up business as usual, except that Forrester and his crutches were watching from the sidelines this time. I wasn't in the mood to play with anyone today, so I took the lead from the start, pacing myself just far enough ahead that there wasn't anyone in sight behind me, so it almost felt like I was skiing the course alone. The powder had gotten better over the past few days, thanks to a weeklong, near-constant light snow, enough so that you didn't have to worry about ice patches or bare spots. You could just ski without thinking about it.

It was about two miles in and I was pretty much on autopilot, thinking about a thesis for an upcoming ten-pager for Hanover's AP lit/comp class. Hers is one of the pitifully few that requires an appreciable amount of thought, which is why I like it so much, and why I actually bother putting a decent amount of effort into her assignments.

Then it happened. With no warning, both my feet started to tingle like I was trying to tightrope across an electric fence. Now, numb feet aren't unheard-of during a Nordic race, especially when the temperature's been hanging out at around minus-ten for the last few days. But once I get going, I rarely even notice the cold unless the temperature really drops down. And this wasn't the gradual chilling down or passing tingle of cold-feet numbness, either.

This was immediate and it hit both feet hard. Suddenly, I had to look down to see what I was skiing on, because I could barely feel my boots around my ankles.

And because I was looking down, trying to figure out what the hell was going on, I didn't see the branch in the middle of the trail until I was on top of it.

It wasn't big, and not seeing it shouldn't have been a problem. Split-second reaction to whatever you feel under you is part of what being a skier is all about. I should have been able to shift weight, take a small jump, and go on my way.

But I couldn't feel what was under my skis.

And I fell.

Fell.

Before I knew what was happening, I was on the ground and rolling to one side of the trail, an ice-crusted twig scraping along my cheek.

To make a long, humiliating story short, I never got it back. I dropped off the trail, out of sight of anyone coming on, to get my bearings and retrieve the ski that flew loose from its binding when I fell. After that first wild jolt that spiked halfway up my legs, the numbness in my feet seemed to settle down. But then it started up in my hands, which made it a real fucking treat to try and hold my poles. By the time I got back onto the trail, the first group had already gone by and the second was closing fast. I got going again, and didn't have any more mishaps, but something was still off. Way off. I held my position from then on but couldn't get up enough speed to catch anyone who'd passed me before. And instead of feeling pumped when I crossed the finish line, which is usual for me, I just felt dead tired. Like a weekend warrior trying to prove something.

And I came in *sixth.*

Freaking pathetic.

I didn't bother stopping once I crossed the finish line, just kept on skiing toward the edge of the field, ignoring the funny look on Coach's face and Jeff and McNeal, who were both among the first five to come in. Jeff did a double take, obviously confused at seeing me finish after him and probably wondering about the frozen blood smeared across my face. He started toward me; I turned away and kept going until I reached the edge.

"Raff!"

I undid my gear, stuffed it haphazardly into my bag, and slung it over my shoulder. Then I put on my sunglasses and took off for the locker room, careful to watch my feet so I wouldn't take another goddamned fall, this time in front of everyone and their brother, and ignoring Jeff's voice trailing after me.

I slammed around the empty locker room, punching lockers until I was breathing hard and my hands were numb *and* bruised. Then I undressed and got into the shower, leaning against the wall and sliding down onto the scummy tile floor, letting the scalding water pound onto me. The scrape on my cheek throbbed as the spray hit it.

"Man, I don't even want to think about the crazy shit you're going to pick up putting your bare ass on that floor."

I snorted, pushing the wet hair out of my eyes, and looked up at Jeff standing in the shower doorway, still completely dressed. "What the hell do you want?"

Jeff shrugged. "Me? Not a thing. Just wondering if you were okay."

"Why the fuck wouldn't I be?" I snapped back.

"Right." Jeff's tone was light, but his eyes looked confused. "Well, anyway, the team shouldn't be up for another ten minutes or so, if you want some time alone or anything."

"Whatever." I closed my eyes again and rested my head on the wall.

"Guess I'll go out and see what they're doing, huh?"

I didn't answer, but he continued.

"When you're done in here, your dad's waiting outside." Jeff's footsteps echoed off the tile, then the heavy outer door banged shut behind him.

Wonderful. The race was an away one, but Dad had driven out for it. Thank God Elise had to work this afternoon.

I hauled my ass out of the shower and got dressed. I was still tired as hell, but my hands and feet felt a little better. Maybe the hot water helped. I hung around and wasted time in the locker room until I heard the rest of the team start coming in, then let myself out the side door.

And almost ran right into my father.

I leaned against the building, hiding behind my sunglasses, not knowing what to say. Dad didn't say much then, either. He just shook his head slowly and handed me his stopwatch, and I closed my hand tightly around it so I wouldn't drop it.

"Not good, son. Not good at all."

I looked at the numbers on the stopwatch face.

No.

Not good at all.

He didn't say anything more until we were home having dinner, and even then he only threw out a few phrases. But they were enough. Dad's not much for yelling when he's pissed, but he has this amazing way of quietly making sure the recipient has no doubt whatsoever about what a disappointment he's been. I've heard him take Eric apart like that for years now. Mistakes don't go down well in this household, and my brother's never been perfect at much of anything.

Until today, it'd been years since I'd given Dad any reason to do the same to me.

I shove my chair away from the desk and start pacing the room again, pissed at my dad. Sure, I'm as disappointed in myself as he is, but I know I screwed up. I don't need to hear it from him, too.

I grab my backpack, toss it on the bed, and stuff a few things inside. I need to get out of this room, or I'll go insane. Dad's gone out, but Mom and Eric are still lurking downstairs, probably waiting to pounce on me as soon as I hit the staircase. I zip the pack closed, then turn the music down—but not off—as a decoy. I ease the door open, shutting it behind me, and sneak down the back steps.

In about three minutes, I'm in the Jeep and heading to Elise's.

Elise lives in one of those rare developments where the houses are more than twenty years old and aren't exact replicas of one another. The cul-de-sacs haven't been plowed yet, and I skid over the drifting snow, past a pseudo-Spanish villa, a futuristic Frank Lloyd Wright knockoff, and a thatched-roof English cottage before sliding into the circular driveway of the brick Tudor. Elise has lived here with her older sister's family since her parents were killed five years ago. I usually won't come over here—her sister has two toddlers who can drive you absolutely up the wall—but the family is over in Vermont for the weekend, and Elise is on her own until Monday.

The only lights I see through the windows are one upstairs and a faint, flickering one in the kitchen. Elise is outlined in the shifting shadows of the kitchen, so I circle around to the side door and let myself in.

The flickering light in the kitchen turns out to be from four fat candles on the table. The overhead lights are off. She's standing at the counter chopping celery, loose hair falling out of her ponytail and curling all over the place in the steam rolling off the pot on the stove. She dumps the celery into the pot and wipes her hands on a towel.

"Hey, you. You're just in time for dinner."

She's a funny one, Elise. Most people I know would make use of an empty house by throwing a party or, at the very least, by ordering takeout. Elise, on the other hand, uses the peace and quiet to cook massive quantities of food. I lift the lid on the pot and inhale the thick curls of steam—chicken noodle. "Just in time? It's ten thirty."

Elise turns toward me, and I can tell she's wondering about the gash on my cheek. Her eyebrows go up, but she doesn't mention it. "Yeah, it had to simmer a few hours. I didn't get started until I got off work." She digs in the fridge, resurfacing with two bottles of Ithaca Nut Brown. She cracks one and hands it to me. "Here, want one? You look like you could use it."

That obvious? I sink into a chair at the big table and down half the beer in one go.

"What the hell are you doing?" I ask. Elise has opened the other beer and dumped it into a bowl. Now she's scooping flour onto it.

"Making bread." She adds some sugar and stirs everything around.

"With beer? Doesn't bread need yeast and shit to rise right?" I don't feel like eating crappy bread with my dinner, and the nagging tingle in my hands and feet isn't helping my mood any.

She calmly finishes mixing and gets out a pan. "Come on, bio genius, you know about fermentation. I'm just using beer to do the job instead of yeast. It's a lot faster, and it's really good."

"With flour, sugar, and beer? I don't know where you're getting your information, but that shit's not going to be any good."

"Tell you what. You can sit here and watch me make this lousy bread and complain, or you can go in and make a fire. We'll eat in there."

"How about I'll make the fire, then I'll complain when the bread turns out lousy?"

"If you like. There's kindling in the basket."

"I know where it is." I take my beer into the living room and do battle with the medieval-style fire screen that blocks the marble fireplace. The thing's iron, weighs about a ton, and crashes to the floor if you so much as breathe on it funny. I get a fire going without too much trouble, then stretch out on the leather couch. I must be even more tired than I thought, because the next thing I know, Elise is shaking me awake and handing me a bowl of soup and a chunk of still-steaming bread.

We eat in silence for a few minutes. The bread's damned good. Nice and moist, with just a touch of nutty taste from the beer. Once in a while, Elise really knows her shit.

"How's your bread?"

"I guess it's okay." No need to swell her ego up too much.

The numbness in my hand spikes, and I almost drop my bowl. I recover it and set it on the floor, then slide off the couch to sit beside it so I don't have to hold it up. What the fuck is going on?

Elise tucks her feet underneath her. "Dane, are you okay?"

"Why wouldn't I be?"

"Ash told me about the meet today."

"When the hell did you talk to Ash?"

"He stopped by the gear shop right before my shift ended. He said you had some trouble. What's up?"

"Nothing's up. I had a bad run. End of story. I don't really feel like talking about it."

"What else is new?" I think I hear Elise mutter under her breath, but I'm not positive. Aloud, she says, "That's fine—I'm sure you can handle it yourself. Just thought I'd ask."

Suddenly, that's not true. Besides being pissed off about the meet and my dad and my time and my stupid-ass fall, I'm getting scared. My body's never failed me like that before, and it freaked me out. I do feel like talking about it.

Guess I'm having a symbiotic moment. The anemone needs a ride on the crab, the hammerhead wants a cleaning from the remora. I close my eyes and let my head fall back into Elise's lap. She twines her fingers into my hair, tugging a little bit.

"I don't know what happened, Lise. One second I was fine, then everything went to hell."

"You still took sixth, didn't you?"

"Like I said. Everything went to hell."

Elise's fingers trace the cut on my cheek, then move to my forehead. "Was it the conditions? I know the powder's been lousy lately. Pretty easy to catch an edge and wipe it out there."

I open my eyes. "It wasn't the powder." That wouldn't be such a big deal. This came from somewhere in *me*.

"You don't always have to be perfect, Dane. No one is."

I don't bother answering that bullshit. She starts to say something else, sighs, and stops. She stares into the fire, flames tossing gold splashes of light across her face. I close my eyes again, and we stay like that for a few minutes as the fire burns lower and sleety snow pounds the windows like buckshot. After a while, she takes the bowls out to the kitchen and I kill the remains of the fire and retrieve my backpack from the hall. Time for bed. I barely make it up the stairs—my toes keep catching on the steps.

Elise has the best bed in the world. It's huge, for one thing, and she's got a featherbed on top of the mattress *and* a down duvet, and those sheets that feel like they're made out of T-shirts. I've christened it NyQuil because it sucks your will to live about five seconds after you lie down on it.

"Dane?" Elise's voice jerks me awake, eyes popping open to stare up at the old-fashioned wooden sign that hangs on the wall above the bed. *DREAM* it says in painted blue letters. "Don't you want to get undressed?"

I've sacked out on top of the duvet, clothes and all.

"Ngh." I would, but my arms and legs feel like someone's held me over a pot of melted lead and dunked me in like the world's biggest candle. I don't think I could move if I were lying in front of a train.

I lie in NyQuil's embrace like a corpse, drifting somewhere between consciousness and oblivion while Elise peels off my boots, fleece, sweater, and jeans. Then she somehow rolls me under the covers. No small feat, since not only do I outweigh her by about fifty pounds, but I also offer no assistance whatsoever.

She finishes getting ready for bed and clicks out the light. A brief blast of cold air invades my cocoon as she gets into bed and curls up behind me.

Her breath wisps against the back of my neck. "I love you." I don't mind her saying that so much, now that she's stopped expecting me to say it back.

I'm about two seconds from full-out dreamland now, no turning back. Going down for the count.

Elise's leg slides over and around mine. As it does, the silky cloth over her knee slips across my bare stomach and down the front of my boxers.

Hey now.

I'm pretty sure it was accidental—Elise usually twines her leg like that when she's ready to fall asleep—but it doesn't matter. A heat rolls over me that has nothing to do with NyQuil's hedonistic bedding.

I turn my head and kiss her cheek, then her neck, and finally both of her closed eyelids. She leans into my kisses like they're water and she's been crawling through the desert for a week.

My body still feels like lead, but there'll be time enough to sleep later. "Come here."

Damn, she's beautiful.

FLORIDA

April 19, 6:20 p.m.

I'm still in the gazebo, watching the sun head toward the horizon. The frogs have started their evening chorus and I've probably missed dinner.

I look down at my legs, pound on my thighs with my fists a couple times, like maybe if I tried hard enough I could get down through the clothes and skin. All the way to the stupid nerves that still won't wake up and do their job.

When the hell are they going to?

As much as I hate to admit it, I wish I could talk to Elise about it. She's a good sounding board. Things seemed to make sense after she and I got done chewing them over together.

For the first time since I got here, thinking about Elise doesn't make me angry.

I just wish she were here.

April 25, 3:30 p.m.

Ash perches on the railing of the front porch. "I still can't believe that cow is your nurse," he snorts, leaning back. "What's she weigh, half a ton?"

He means Letitia, whom he met this morning. I want him to shut up. How did I never notice how obnoxious Ash can be? He's already been a jerk to Isaac, who saw me here on the porch and came to join us because he thought I was watching birds again. I ignore him and turn back to Jeff, who's lounging on the wooden swing. "How long you guys down for?"

I got the surprise of my life when Jeff and Ash showed up this morning. I've been stuck in this place so long I'd almost forgotten that things like spring break still exist for some of the world.

"We'll start back from Fort Lauderdale on Friday," Jeff says. "We're driving over there to meet McNeal and Cabot at the hotel later tonight."

"How's Forrester doing, anyway?" I'd almost forgotten about Cabot, too.

"Okay, not great," Ash says. "He's off the crutches now, but he still really limps when he gets tired."

Perspective's everything, isn't it? From where I'm sitting now, that does sound great. I wish GBS were as quick to bounce back from as an Achilles repair. How is that fair?

I change the subject. "I can't believe you came this far out of your way just to visit." The veggie ranch isn't exactly on the route to anyplace interesting. Besides losing a day of their vacation, stopping here also meant Jeff and Ash had to drive down from New York on their own instead of going with the rest of the guys.

"Yeah, it was Jeff's idea—," Ash starts to say, but Jeff stops him with a look.

"We just couldn't resist," Jeff says, turning around and pretending to eye the building behind us with the gawking stare of a tourist. "The vacation guides all list the hospital as a must-see attraction." He grins at me, then turns serious. "You think we'd come all the way down to Florida and not see you?"

"Well, I'm glad you did." Until he turned up, I hadn't realized how much I'd missed Jeff.

Ash, on the other hand, isn't doing much for me. Drumming his heels against the railing posts, he pulls his sunglasses off and gives me an appraising look. "How much longer you stuck in that thing?" he asks.

He's referring—of course—to the wheelchair. Before I can think of the cleverest way to respond to a question I can't answer, Jeff breaks in.

"More importantly, when are you getting out of here, Raff? Everyone's asking."

I wonder if Elise has asked. I dodge the question. "Hard to say. Not long, though."

"Well, I can't wait to have you back." Jeff suddenly gets up.

"Almost forgot," he calls back as he jogs down the front steps to the parking lot. "Just a second."

I glance over at Ash, who raises his eyebrows and shrugs. "Beats me," he says. Across the lot, we watch Jeff rummage through the trunk of the car. He pulls out his backpack, grabs something, and comes back.

"Here you go." He sets a pile of cards in my lap. "From everyone back home."

I glance through the stack of envelopes as casually as I can. A lot of the handwriting is familiar, but it quickly becomes clear that the small, slightly slanted script I'm looking for isn't among them. "Thanks. I'll read them later." I push the pile down between my leg and the wheelchair armrest.

"You guys know what Elise is up to over break?" Damn. So much for the promise I'd made myself.

"Stayed up north. She's snowboarding over at Smugglers'," Jeff says.

"With who?" I hate the jealousy boiling up in me.

"Her sister, I think." Jeff looks curious. "Have you talked to her at all since you've been gone?"

"No." I try to sound indifferent.

"We were surprised you guys split when you did," Ash interjects. "Seemed like a weird time for you to break up with her."

"You know how it goes," I say, trying to cover my surprise. Is that what Elise told everyone? I broke up with her? Why would she say that? "How's she doing, anyway? She seeing anyone these days?"

"Not right now," Jeff says quickly. "She's been keeping pretty busy."

"But that'll be changing before long if Jeff has anything to say about it." Ash grins at Jeff. "Right?"

What? I whip my head around to stare at Jeff, who's turned scarlet.

"Damn it, Ash," he says quietly.

"What?" Ash says. "What's the big deal? Raff doesn't care; he ditched the girl, right? And you were going to tell him today, anyway. ..." He breaks off, his gaze bouncing back and forth between Jeff and me. We're staring, paralyzed, at each other. "Right," he says uneasily, jumping down from the railing. "I'll just go feed my pet tumor now." He pulls a lighter and a pack of cigarettes from the pocket of his khaki shorts and disappears.

I snap out of it first. "Tell me what?" I ask, making sure to sound like I'm only half-interested in whatever he's going to say.

Jeff sighs hard and closes his eyes. "This wasn't how I planned to bring this up," he says, shaking his head.

"What? You sleeping with Elise or something?" I don't know how the hell I'm keeping my voice so calm as I say that.

"No!" Jeff's eyes pop open. "No, not at all. I've just been thinking about asking her out."

"What about Angelica?"

"Angie? We were history a month and a half ago."

"She break up with you over what happened at your party?"

Jeff shakes his head. "She should have, but no. After I apologized, she was ready to take me back, but I couldn't do it. Not after what I'd done, and definitely not after I admitted to myself that I'd been with her for all the wrong reasons. I never had any business getting involved with Angie in the first place."

I take a deep breath. "And now you want to start something

with Elise. How do those reasons compare?"

"Not even in the same time zone," Jeff says. A weird look comes over his face and his eyes go all soft. "Dane, you're my oldest friend in the world. You know I've been absolutely in love with Elise since before we even started high school."

My fingernails are digging little crescents into my palms. In *love* with her? What else didn't I know about? "What does she have to say about all this?" I ask. I know Elise has always gotten along well with Jeff, but that was just because they both had me in common. Right?

"She doesn't know."

"You haven't said anything to her yet?"

"No. Hell, I don't even know if she'd say yes in the first place. I guess I kind of wanted to run it by you before I did anything," he adds. "I mean, is it cool with you if I do?"

I can't be having this conversation. Okay, Jeff's always had sort of a thing for Elise, but I absolutely never expected this.

I sit in a daze as he keeps talking. I wish I'd brought the binoculars out so I'd at least have something to hide behind. If I have to look at Jeff's earnest, oblivious face much longer, I'm going to punch something.

He's still talking. "I mean, normally I'd never even consider asking out a friend's ex, but since you broke up with her, I figured you probably don't care."

I break out of my trance. "She told you that?"

"Of course not. She hasn't said anything, other than that the two of you weren't together anymore. But it was pretty clear who got tired of who," Jeff says. He puts his hands on his knees and leans forward on the swing.

"Everyone knows you always meant way more to Elise than she did to you." He tilts his head. "Weird, isn't it? To me—and probably most of the free world—she's like on this pedestal, almost too good to be real, you know? But to the one person she really loved, she wasn't ever anything special. Her bad luck for falling for the only guy in the world who doesn't need anything from anyone. Right, buddy?"

He shakes his head again, bemused, as the bottom silently drops out of my stomach.

April 25, 6:05 p.m.

Jeff and Ash have been gone an hour before I remember the cards stuffed in my chair. As I throw the pile—unopened—into my bottom dresser drawer, one envelope falls to the floor. When I finally manage to pick it up, I almost throw it in the trash but stop when I feel something stiff inside. I turn the envelope over. There's nothing written on it. After a few tries, I get it open. There's no letter inside.

Just a picture from Walden Pond.

April 26, 5:20 p.m.

"You're doing it wrong."

"I am not."

"Yeah, you are. You need more flour than that."

Carissa ignores me and reaches for the chocolate-chip bag. As she squints at the recipe printed on the back, I dip a spoon into the flour and launch a white shower into her hair.

"Hey!" She retaliates with a handful of chocolate chips. I catch some in my mouth.

"Thanks. At least I get to eat something before you destroy the rest of the supplies."

"Shut up, New York. You're not here to provide commentary." Carissa glares at me and adds some more flour to the bowl.

"No? Enlighten me, please. Why am I here, again?" I ask, trying to locate all the chips that landed in my chair so I won't find them melted to my ass later on.

"You're my guinea pig, of course. You'll eat one first, then I'll know if they're safe for human consumption."

"Let me spare you the suspense," I tell her. "They won't be."

Baking cookies certainly wasn't *my* idea. Carissa's the one who got bored, opted to play Rachael Ray in the OT kitchen, and targeted me as the victim she'd force to accompany her.

And I do mean force. The little snot took Joel's binoculars hostage and threatened to drop them in the pond and frame me for it if I didn't come keep her company.

So here I am in the tiny kitchen where Joel and Casey help patients relearn how to cook and stuff, watching Carissa mix up what I can safely predict will be the worst batch of cookies ever. She measures her ingredients by the handful. This girl would be absolutely deadly in a chemistry lab.

Oddly enough, I don't really mind hanging out, even though I'm doing so under threat of blackmail. I find her to be strangely amusing, in an irritating sort of way.

And right now I'll do just about anything to avoid thinking about yesterday's conversation with Jeff.

As if she's read my thoughts and decided to mess with me, Carissa asks, "So you actually got some company yesterday, huh? Friends from home?"

"Uh-huh," I say, hoping she'll leave it at that. Yeah, right.

"One of them seemed pretty decent."

"You mean the dark-haired one?" Girls usually take to Ash pretty quickly.

Carissa makes a disgusted noise. "What, Mr. Back-to-Nature-in-Designer-Clothes-and-Hair-Products? I could tell he was a complete sausage even before he opened his obnoxious mouth." She dumps the rest of the chocolate chips into the batter, doesn't bother to stir them, and starts tossing spoonfuls onto a cookie sheet.

"I meant the one who wants to ask out your girlfriend."

I focus on shoving back the tight, furious feeling that's been trying to slither up my insides since yesterday. "That seems like a decent thing for a friend to do? How did you know about that, anyway?"

Carissa takes the cookies over to the oven. "I was eaves-dropping, of course. I have to do my living vicariously, remember?"

"Right, how could I forget?" I smash the wooden spoon down on two stray chips left in the mixing bowl, imagining that they're Jeff and Elise. "And I don't know why it surprised me that you'd prefer the one who basically asked my permission to stab me in the back."

"Oh, grow up. You and Eskimo chick—"

"Elise."

"Okay, whatever. You and Elise don't exist anymore. So let her be with someone who actually appreciates her. Your friend seems to care about her. And you, for that matter, not that I can figure out why. Nobody who's planning to stab someone in the back asks their permission first. Besides, I don't think he'd even have thought about asking her out if he knew what really happened with you and her."

"And you do?"

The oven door bangs shut and Carissa sits down across from me again. "You weren't the one who broke up with her, were you?"

I force myself to unclench my teeth. "How'd you make that brilliant assumption?"

"Easy. You're hurt."

"I am not!"

"Right. Okay, you're pissed. If you'd broken up with her, you'd be indifferent. And you'd have thrown away that wooden bird she gave you or stuffed it in a drawer somewhere instead of hauling it down here with you." She leans her chair back with the self-satisfied look of someone who's just won a Nobel Prize.

"All right, well done. My girlfriend took off after I got sick and just before I got sent down here." The raw edges of the memory take a few bites before I can stop them. "No big screaming deal—just proves yet again that you can't trust people."

"It does not." Carissa lets her chair thump back down. "If you were as much of an asshole back home as you are now, there's no question why she ditched you, New York."

Blowing up in front of Carissa would only amuse her. "It's a moot point, anyway. Elise and I were just a casual thing. It's not like she ever did a hell of a lot for me in the first place. So drop it, okay? Unless you want to see how much of an asshole I can be."

"Whatever you say," she smirks. "Your sob story's getting boring, anyhow."

"You're the one who brought it up!"

"Yeah, but I thought it would be more interesting." Carissa starts to gather up the mess of cookie ingredients littering the table. I reach out and stop her.

"Wait. I'm going to make a batch, too."

"But I already made enough," she says, checking the timer on the oven. "They'll be done in seven minutes."

"And, sorry to tell you, they're going to be about as good as the Whack-Offs' last batch of brownies."

"Hey!"

The Whack-Off Society is not some strange club for the socially minded masturbator. In actuality, it's the very unofficial name of this OT cooking group that Casey and Joel hold a couple times a week. I've never attended one, but their exploits are legendary around here. Depending on the capabilities of the week's participants, they might make something as simple as those cheater tubes of premixed cookie dough that you just whack slices off and toss onto a cookie sheet (whack-off cookies, as Casey has christened them).

Sometimes, though, the stuff they come up with is surprisingly good. Last week, Casey's group managed a perfectly decent spaghetti carbonara (I know this because Joel sneaked into the kitchen and stole two platefuls for us). But for Joel's group, last week's showing was remarkably poor—a single pan of brownies so charred that Joel had to pry them loose with a screwdriver. Undaunted, he used a hammer to break the brownies into pieces, had his group decorate them with sequins and glitter (Isaac was thrilled), then sprayed them with varnish and declared them paperweights. One mysteriously turned up on my dresser, but I've yet to pinpoint the perpetrator.

"Actually," I say, grinning at her, "maybe Casey and Joel have some room in their next session. Just think—you could learn to use a measuring cup and everything!"

"Did anyone ever tell you you're not remotely funny?" Carissa says. "Fine, make your own cookies. Be a slave to the recipe."

"I'll do that," I say, mixing up the second round of dough.

She's unusually quiet for the next few minutes, contenting herself with trying to sneak extra ingredients into my mixing bowl. Finally, I stab her hand with the wooden spoon. "Knock it off. Just because you don't use measurements doesn't mean I can't."

"Oh, all right." Carissa sniffs. She watches me in silence for a few more seconds.

Then, "So your family's coming down pretty soon, huh?"

There's no such thing as personal privacy around here. "Yeah, in a couple days," I tell her.

"How long since you saw them last?"

"Almost two months, I guess."

"Well, you must be pretty excited, right?" We both jump as the timer blasts. Between fanning smoke with a dish towel and cursing when she grabs the hot cookie sheet with a torn oven mitt, Carissa thankfully doesn't notice my lack of reply to her question.

"You want me to put yours in?" she asks.

"No, I can get it." I balance the full cookie sheet carefully on my lap and wheel over to the oven. Carissa watches me appraisingly.

"Not bad, New York," she says when I get the cookies in and the oven door shut without burning myself or dropping anything. "Hate to admit it, but I think you might actually be starting to get yourself back together."

"My top half, anyway." I wheel back to the table and start cleaning up.

"Hey, half a body's a hell of a lot better than anything happening on my home front," Carissa says, swiping a dishrag across the table.

"Your dad's still the same, huh?"

She snorts. "We're all as stagnant as ever. Unless you ask my mom, of course." She fires the rag across the room into the sink, scowling.

"She won't let either of us go. At least your parents treat you like an adult, letting you do your thing down here on your own."

Her next words are almost whispered. "I wish he'd just hurry up and die."

I raise an eyebrow. "You know, you constantly call me an asshole, but you're not much better."

She doesn't deny it, just shrugs and starts rattling dishes in the sink. "We'd be better off, New York, and you know it. More importantly, he'd be better off, too. He really would."

"What're you going to do, kill him?" The words come out without thinking, but Carissa doesn't even blink.

"Maybe." She's talking to the sink, but she sounds dead serious.

"Come on." I look at her back.

She turns around and leans against the sink. "Do you know how easy it would be?" she says.

"What, to kill your dad?" This conversation is taking a turn for the weird, even for her. "Let me guess—you're planning on doing him in with a pillow or something? Sorry, I think someone would figure it out."

Carissa crosses her arms. "I'm serious."

"So am I. Don't think I'm going to come visit you in prison." I'm trying to lighten things up a little, but she doesn't even crack a smile.

"All I'd have to do is turn off that dumb alarm. Nobody would ever know a thing." I immediately know what she means.

She's talking about the machine that breathes for Robert. Because I was on one myself for a while, I know they have this alarm hooked up to them that goes off whenever something goes wrong and blocks the airflow. Usually it happens when junk builds up in your airway, and the alarm alerts someone that they need to suction it out so you won't choke on it. There are some other alarms, too, but for some inexplicable reason, the volume on all of them can be turned down or even completely off. Anyone who's paid attention can see how it's done.

Carissa's probably just talking, but I can't help arguing her strategy a little. "It wouldn't work, though. Once you turned it off, who knows how long you'd have to wait around for something to go wrong."

She laughs humorlessly. "You haven't seen how fast my dad's lungs fill up. Someone's in suctioning him every five minutes, at least." She's right. Robert's alarm does go off at all hours. It used to keep me awake at first, but now I don't even notice it.

"Besides," she continues, "that new nurse who replaced Sara on the night shift is a complete flake. Between her smoke breaks and her text messaging, she probably wouldn't notice if I charged past her desk with a shotgun over my shoulder. Besides that, she never remembers to call respiratory to suction my dad like she's supposed to."

"But what about your mom? She's here all the time."

"Yeah. There is that." Carissa turns back to the dishes without further comment.

My cookies turn out a little flat, but they're a whole lot better than Carissa's, which have an undeniably smoky taste to them (she made me try one). We split them up on two paper plates to eat later, then Carissa takes off to kick a ball around before it gets dark.

When I wheel past the therapists' office, the light's still on, which is unusual but not unheard-of this late in the day. I remember Joel saying something earlier today about he and Anya staying late to catch up on some paperwork. I don't see Joel any-where, but Anya's there, bent over her desk with her back to me. I decide to unload some cookies on them, especially Carissa's.

I slip silently into the office with the same stealth I've been practicing on the animals outside. I'm getting pretty good. She doesn't even notice as I wheel up behind her and grab her shoulder.

Anya whirls around in her chair, one arm flying up as if to protect herself from a punch. Her blue eyes are huge and her face the color of a fish's underside. I barely manage to duck in time to avoid getting clobbered.

"Hey, it's just me," I say, confused at her violent reaction.

"Dane," she says, breathing hard. "What are you doing here?"

"We made—I mean, I was just bringing you guys some cookies. I didn't mean to ..." My voice trails off. Anya still looks way more scared than she should. I start to ask her if she's okay, but then Joel comes into the office carrying a stack of patient charts.

"Hey, Dane, here for some extra OT?" he says with a laugh.

"Looks like he already did some," Anya breaks in, pointing at the plate of cookies still in my lap. Her voice sounds like she's forcing it to be light. I leave half the cookies with them and get out of there, completely confused.

What the hell was that about?

April 26, 6:30 p.m.

I'm throwing rocks into the pond and thinking over what Carissa said about why Elise left me.

Not that her input should be cause for much pondering—I could buy Carissa front-row seats to the World Cup finals and she'd still find fifty reasons to call me an asshole.

I did lie to her today, though. When I said that Elise never really did anything for me. That's not true. Especially the morning after that last night we spent together.

The morning when I guess she saved my life.

UPSTATE NEW YORK

February 23, 6:34 a.m.

Thin, gray light is struggling through the window when Elise finally wakes up. She rolls over and drops a kiss on my bare shoulder, the thin silver ring in her right nipple grazing my arm. "Morning."

I've been awake and silently freaking out for over an hour. Something is fucking wrong with me.

I've never been much of an early morning kisser—or talker for that matter—so Elise doesn't notice anything strange when I don't answer her. She slips out of bed, pulling the covers back over me but missing the desperate message I'm trying to send her with my eyes, and tugs on her pale green pajama pants and a tank top. Her dark hair's loose and tumbling all around her face.

"I'll go see what I can scare up for breakfast, okay? Be right back." She slides into the old pair of flip-flops she uses as slippers and pads out the door. I can't follow her, because I can't move.

At all.

I thought I felt like a lead Popsicle last night. That was nothing, absolutely nothing to the utter dead weight now lying grounded in the spot where my body used to live.

Why the fuck can't I move?

Okay, maybe we need to start small. How about we just move the legs? No? A hand? A finger? One lousy damned finger?

One by one, my brain orders body parts to wake the hell up and perform their respective duties. And one by one, responses come zooming back up the neuronal freeways. Screw you. Misfire in the wiring maybe, but we're not moving. Save your breath.

Speaking of breath, something's going really wrong there, too, and I don't think it's just because I'm terrified. Sometime during the night, my whole face went pins and needles. The throbbing woke me right up, and that's when I discovered I couldn't move anything except my eyes. I tried to wake up Elise, but suddenly there was a boulder sitting on my chest. I couldn't get enough breath to talk any louder than a whisper, and she sleeps way too heavy to hear that.

So I lay there, right beside Elise—God, some of the time she was even touching me—panic spiraling through my head with no way to let itself out.

And now that she's finally woken up, she's taken off for the damned kitchen.

And it's getting even harder to get air into my lungs.

By the time she comes back, I'm gasping silently, fighting like hell to drag in oxygen and force my chest to expand enough to let me breathe. She doesn't notice. She hops onto the foot of the bed. "Dane? You alive?"

For the moment. Come on, Elise.

"Come on, wake up, slug. There's hot chocolate and croissants downstairs." She shakes my leg.

Elise! Look the fuck up!

Black dots dance in front of my eyes.

"You're not going to sleep all day, are you?"

My entire body is on fire.

"Okay—if you want to grab a little more shut-eye, go ahead. I'll be downstairs."

No! Don't leave!

I have to get her attention. But how? I can't talk, can't breathe. Hell, in about two seconds, I might be dead. Finally, in absolute, futile desperation, I try one last time to scream through my half-open mouth that won't move.

It doesn't work, of course. All that comes out is a thick, strangled hiss, like a tire going flat.

But somehow, amazingly, it's enough. Elise stops in the doorway and turns around. "Hey, you are awake." She crosses back to the bed and sits down again. This time, thank God, at the head.

But that last effort has sucked out anything remaining that I might have had. The black spots are spreading, and I just can't make my lungs work anymore.

"Dane?" Elise finally pulls down the blanket that's been hiding most of my face from her.

"Dane!"

Elise's hand under my chin, tilting my head back, listening at my mouth.

Elise on her cell phone, her words fast and snapping like ice.

Elise kneeling over me, her mouth on mine, forcing in air that burns as it goes down.

A blue red, flashing glow blends with the gray light from the window, reflecting off Elise's face.

The last thing I see before the blackness closes over me.

FLORIDA

April 26, 7:45 p.m.

Splash.

I'm still out here tossing rocks.

That was the last time I saw Elise with her hair down.

Splash.

The last time I felt her mouth against mine.

Splash.

The last time she made things all right.

Splash. Splash. Splash.

If I was such an asshole, then why did she even bother in the first place?

April 29, 10:32 a.m.

My father takes off his wire frames and polishes them on his vest. Replacing them, he folds his arms and gives Anya an appraising look. "I imagine that when you're something of a neophyte, you may not be as aggressive with your patients' treatment as perhaps you ought. How long did you say you've been a therapist?"

The Happy Household of Rafferty has officially arrived. Someone kill me. Please. Or at least leave me alone long enough to find some oxygen tubing and hang myself with it.

In all fairness, it didn't get bad until today. Eric and Mom arrived yesterday, and we had a surprisingly good time together. Mom's gotten deep into a new book project since I've been gone, which gave us plenty to talk about. And Eric's the same as ever. He gave me a lengthy update on my turtle (who he's afraid of but is still watching for me) and made me watch his latest couple karate katas. He's better than I remember. Mom seems proud of him, too. I took him out on one of my predusk wildlife hunts last night, and he got to see an armadillo for the first time. Four of them, actually—a mother and her babies. He almost died laughing when he saw them, said they looked like walking bowling balls. Crazy kid. I was bummed when he had to leave for the hotel with Mom.

Then this morning dawned, and Professor John Rafferty made his appearance. Apparently he's obtained degrees in nursing, medicine, and physical therapy from somewhere since I saw him last, because he spent his first hour here standing over the nurses and offering his opinions on everything.

And he hasn't stopped yet, as evidenced by his presence in my PT session. Families usually aren't encouraged to watch therapy (Anya thinks they're distracting), and Mom got the hint and took Eric to town for a few hours. Dad, however, insisted on sitting in. Since he'd come from so far away, Anya made an exception and let him come for the last half hour, a decision she's no doubt already regretting.

If I weren't already so annoyed myself, it would be almost funny to watch Anya try and answer Dad's critiques of her experience and clinical expertise without clenching her teeth. She forces a smile.

"Almost four years, Mr. Rafferty."

Dad frowns thoughtfully. "Hmm. Four years ... and that's with what, a bachelor's degree?"

"A doctorate," Anya answers over her shoulder, which shuts him up momentarily, then turns back to me. "Ready to try again?"

"Sure." I'm sitting on one of those huge, inflatable balls you see in gyms or on Pilates commercials, trying to keep my balance without Anya helping me. It makes my muscles burn like hell (it's a lot harder than it looks), but it's really been helping my balance and torso strength. This time, I hold myself steady for almost four minutes before Anya has to catch me.

"Fantastic!" Anya says, slapping me five. I'm psyched, too.

That beats my previous record by over a minute. I wipe sweat off my forehead, and glance across the room at my dad when I hear him clear his throat. He doesn't look impressed.

"Aren't you going to do anything on your feet, Dane? Come on, show me what you've been doing down here for the past two months."

I look at Anya. She raises her eyebrows at me. "Your choice," she mouths silently. We worked on standing in the parallel bars during the first half of our session, and I was pretty tired out from it even before my dad came in. Even when I'm fresh it always takes me a few tries to pull myself up, and Anya has to help hold me when I get there.

But, tired out or not, I know my dad well enough to know he'll never let it go until I give him what he wants to see. So I might as well get it over with.

"Okay, let's give it a try," I tell Anya quietly. She holds the ball while I slide off into my wheelchair, then I take myself over between the parallel bars. Anya brings a stool and sits in front of me.

"Can't he do this by himself?" My dad has walked across the room and is leaning on the opposite end of the bars, watching. He addresses Anya as though I'm not there. She starts to answer him. I know what she's going to say, that no, I can't stand up without her helping me. So I interrupt her before she can finish.

"Right, I'll do it myself, Anya. You don't need to help."

Anya raises her eyebrows, starts to shake her head, then stops and shrugs. She stays in front of me but uses her feet to wheel her stool back to give me some more room. I'm on my own.

I try to tune out my dad's watching-a-zoo-performance stare

and narrow my focus in on my body and what I desperately want it to do. I breathe deep and push my body forward until I'm sitting on the very edge of the wheelchair. Then I reach up to the parallel bars and grab one in each hand. I've never done this without help from Anya. I concentrate, remembering the sequence of steps that we always go through to get me standing: plant both feet on the ground, as far back as possible; shift weight forward through my legs. At this point, she usually pulls my hips forward and up, giving just a little extra power to my upward push. I try and give the extra push myself this time, and send my glutes and quad muscles the message that they need to contract hard and long enough to let me straighten my legs so they can support my weight.

It doesn't work. I make it halfway into standing, but it's my arms that are doing the work, pulling me up, instead of my legs pushing me where I want to go. I sink back into the chair.

"Come on, Dane. Focus." Brilliant words of encouragement from guess who. I glance at my father's intense face, nod, and quickly turn my gaze back to my feet. I try again. Then again.

The logical part of my brain knows this is pointless, absolutely stupid. I know I can't stand up by myself. Particularly not at the end of an hour-long workout, when my muscles are thrashed and sweat's dried all over me in salty streaks. But I can't stop. Anya's whispering to me, telling me to ease up, to listen to my body. I ignore her.

"Hey, Dane, you look wiped!" Joel's walked into the gym. "Maybe you should take a breather, huh?" He looks over at Anya, who shrugs, her face resigned.

Now Dad's standing over me, first yelling out encouragement, then anger, and finally disgust. "This is ridiculous, Dane. I'm not asking for much, here. Just stand up already!"

His words break Anya out of her silence. "Mr. Rafferty, you *are* asking too much. Dane can't stand just yet—not alone, anyway. And he's tired now," she adds, eyeing my flushed, sweaty face and trembling legs.

My father's face turns red at her words. "You're telling me that after almost two months of rehab, my son can't handle a simple task like standing up? Just what have you been wasting your time on, then?" His glare arcs around the room, skewering Anya and Joel in turn, then homing in on me. "Did you know that most people with your disorder are back on their feet by now? Do you think I raised you to *fail*?" He spits the word at me. "Now get up!"

Anya moves forward to stop me, but she doesn't even need to. I haven't got anything left. My arms and legs are shaking, sweat drenches my face and body, and I'm not going to make it onto my feet. I can't look at my father's face, so I stare straight ahead as his verbal assault washes over me like sewage. He yells right over both Anya's and Joel's attempts to break in, telling me how useless I am, how disappointing, demanding to know how I've been wasting these last two months instead of focusing on getting back on my game.

And I snap. Reaching down with shaking hands, I slam the wheelchair footrests back into place, haul my legs onto them, and make for the door to the hallway like it's a *Titanic* lifeboat.

I'm dimly aware of voices—Joel's coldly restrained, Anya's fiery and not even trying to sound polite, my father's still yelling after me. They fade behind me as I retreat down the hallway to the outside doors. I'm going too fast. I don't care. The refrigerated indoor air dissolves into sticky, hot wind as I shove my wheelchair down the ramp and onto the pond path, ignoring the nearly blinding glare from the cloudless sky and the gnawing burn in my shoulders. Trying to ignore the burning behind my eyes.

It's not working. I can barely see the path in front of me, and the outline of the pond looks faint and wavy.

I make it all the way to the wooden pavilion on the far edge before my arms give out. I fold them on the railing and drop my head into them. Then I just sit there, listening to the wind rustling the cattails and the ragged sound of my own breathing that's shaking my shoulders and making my chest hurt.

Footsteps creak on the planks behind me. I don't look up, even when someone puts their hands on my shoulders.

"It's hard, isn't it?" It's Anya. Her voice is a lot softer than usual, almost the same gentle tone she used the other day with Carissa's mom.

I don't trust my voice to answer her, so I just leave my head buried in my arms. I shrug her hands off my shoulders.

But she puts them back. This time she squeezes a little harder. I don't want her to touch me. I want to tell her to get lost, to leave me the hell alone, to go find someone else to bother. If she doesn't leave, I'm afraid I'm going to break in front of her.

"Dane, I know he's your dad, but you absolutely can't listen to him on this. You have every reason to be proud of how far you've come, especially in these last few weeks." Anya's hand trails up and down my back, rubbing in small circles. "And you still have a lot more progress to make. We're not even close to being done with each other yet."

I try to laugh. It doesn't quite work. I should have realized way before now that I was only kidding myself.

"It's pointless. He doesn't want anything that's broken." I

whisper the words so quietly that I don't even know if she heard me.

But it's true. My father has no use for anything suboptimal unless he can use it to make some sort of educational point. Like the time when I was six and Dad and I came across a porcupine that had been hit on the road in front of our house. It was broken but not quite dead, had just enough life left in it to scrabble its legs weakly against the gravel as we approached. Dad knelt down beside it, studied it momentarily, then motioned me closer. I inched forward, thinking he was going to send me to find a rock or something to put it out of its misery. Wrong.

"Look, Dane." I looked down at the porcupine. Red stained the ground around it and a lot of its quills were broken. It was shaking. Dad pointed. "This is your lucky day. You don't usually get to see these guys up close, and they're fascinating. See how the quills are barbed there on the ends?"

I nodded, swallowing hard. The porcupine was making tiny squeaking noises. Its eyes rolled frantically.

Dad continued the biology lesson for another five minutes, then got up and said it was time to go have lunch.

"But what are we going to do with him?" I asked. The porcupine was still alive.

Dad shrugged. "Nothing. He'll die soon. The crows will take care of things after that."

"I know, but—"

"Dane, that's just the way it works." Dad sounded like he was starting to lose patience. "Not everything is strong enough to survive. Look at it this way. At least you got to learn something today." He turned and went into the house, and that was that.

Now I'm the porcupine with the fascinating quill structure. Of educational interest, but otherwise inconsequential.

Anya hasn't said anything more, but she's still rubbing my back. At least she doesn't lie and try to tell me that I'm wrong. I haven't lifted my head. Then I feel her lean over and hear her voice beside my ear.

"I don't care what your dad says, and I don't give a damn what he thinks. You are not broken."

I look up then, wiping my eyes quickly as I do. Looking out at the pond instead of at Anya, I finally ask her the question that's been chewing on every corner of my brain.

"Tell me the truth, okay? Am I ever going to get back to the way I was? Am I ever going to walk again?"

From the corner of my eye, I watch Anya twist her silver necklace around her finger. Around and around until the chain almost cuts into her throat. The hot breeze blows strands of red hair across her face. She looks angry, but not at me.

"I don't know, Dane. I really don't know."

May 1

Talk to family? Forget it.

Talk to anyone here? No way.

Go to PT or OT? Like hell.

Wheel around aimlessly, agonizing over what the hell's the point of any of it anymore?

We have a winner.

And that's what I've been doing for the past two days. When I haven't been hiding out in my bed (where I've spent an inordinate amount of time), I'm outside, not even bothering to take the binoculars with me, just keeping on the move so nobody will find me and try to make me talk to them.

Yes, I know. Pathetic.

But it's bad enough having all this shit playing on repeat in my head. What possible good would it do to further dismember a dead horse by rehashing things with anyone else? Not that anyone seems to get that, of course. Everyone's just dying to help, and the fact that I've been ignoring them all isn't doing anything to slow the onslaught.

Letitia: "Come on, sweet pea, get up. You camp in that bed any longer and your backside gonna root itself right to the mattress."

Joel: "We don't have to do any OT stuff today, Dane. Just come outside with me for a while."

Anya: "Don't listen to him, Dane. Don't let him take away everything we've—you've—accomplished. Trust me, he doesn't have a clue. Families never do."

"Get your ass moving, will you? You're starting to look about as good as my dad." Take a guess. I actually did stop in to see Robert once when nobody was around; I don't know why. You can imagine how much help he was.

At least my family's gone, thank God. After the shit storm exploded the other day, they headed over to the Gulf coast to sightsee for a few days. Allegedly, they'll stop back afterward. When Dane's in a better frame of mind, I believe, is how my parents put it. Bullshit. I can pretty much guarantee I'll be getting a phone call any day now, telling me they decided to head on home. Which is absolutely fine by me. I wouldn't have a thing to say even if they did come back.

Clearly, I wouldn't have anything remotely impressive to show them, either.

That's why I can't forgive Anya and Joel. Them, and all the rest of the whole fucking rehab joke. They suck you into this weird little hospital world, this warped microcosm, an imitation of real life where everyone gets excited for you and makes a huge deal over any sort of progress, no matter how tiny. And they make you start to believe their shit, too.

But then you forget that nobody in the world outside measures success with the same gauge. And when your friends or your family come to see what you can do, they don't see how hard and how long you've been fighting, day after day. To rebuild yourself piece by painful piece back toward something remotely resembling what you used to be.

All they see is you still sitting in a wheelchair, when the textbooks and Web sites all say that *most* people who get Guillain-Barré should be able to walk by now.

It's finally hit me. I may not be able to win this one. Dane Rafferty, who's never had to settle for being second best at *anything* if he didn't want to, just might fall into that 25 percent failure rate.

Just might never ski again.

And if I'm not the best, then who the hell am I?

So I'm done with all of it, including therapy. Especially therapy. It wouldn't make any damned difference, anyway.

They all keep talking, though. Trying to spin some cotton-candy web of shit to give me the magic jump start. But they don't matter. If there's one thing I can do, it's tune things out. ...

UPSTATE NEW YORK

February 23, 7:45 a.m.

"Eighteen-year-old white male, presenting with respiratory arrest of indeterminate etiology."

"Heart rate 187, BP 154 over 98."

"Severe cyanosis of lips and nail beds. Capillary refill time five seconds."

"No voluntary motor response aside from sporadic bilateral eye movement. Semiconscious. Minimal response to painful stimuli."

I'm not here.

My body may be lying on this cot in this ambulance that's skidding all over the ice-glazed road, but I'm not. The old guy in the blue jacket may be shoving air down into my lungs through that mask with the bag attached to it, but it's not me who feels the tearing ache as my chest is forced outward again and again. The ache I feel is in my calves as I crouch in the cattails at the edge of the reservoir, knee-deep in mud and leeches, an hour of silent waiting finally rewarded as the kingfisher I've been staking out through my binoculars makes a spectacular dive off the tree branch. He arrows into the water, disappearing beneath the surface, then rises into the air again, a thrashing fish glinting silver in his beak.

"Let's maintain that airway. Keep bagging him, Keith."

I'm in my canoe in the middle of the river, the slow-moving one where we watched the eastern newts mating. *Notophthalamus viridescens.* One's brittle, slippery legs clamped around the other's body almost tight enough to pierce through, making skin and eyes bulge. Like there could never be any kind of sharing without one inflicting pain, one silently enduring it. Taking when they need to whatever they can get from each other.

"What'd the girl say his name was?"
"Dave, I think."
"Dave? Can you keep your eyes open for me? I want you to look at me."

Orion fighting with Taurus. Cassiopeia and Gemini and the Pleiades whirling over me. Elise in the front of the canoe, paddle resting across her knees, head tilted back to the sky and the night. A soft yelp escapes her lips, betraying the fact that she's just spotted a shooting star. *Estrella fugaz,* she calls it—something random she picked up from some long-dead Ecuadorian grandmother.

"I'm getting nothing here. Let's get him on the vent."

Like that night last February. When we set our alarms for 3:00 a.m. and met to watch the Leonids. Biggest meteor shower ever. The night was bone-chewing bitter—fifteen below, easy—but it didn't matter. Elise brought a scalding-hot Thermos of cocoa and we lay in the ice-crusted snow on the shore of Tooley Pond, stuffed into huge parkas like Mr. Stay-Puft gone Gore-Tex. Parked the Jeep close with the key on and the music pulsing softly with the strings and synthesizers and eerie chorals of Enigma's *LSD* album. Music that would be sensual if you were grinding against each other on a sweaty dance floor, but out here simply providing a dreamlike choreography for the icy streaking tails of the meteors. The stars crashed and burned their way across the sky above us, so beautiful that you completely forgot you were freezing your ass off.

Until you tried to get up, and your leg muscles couldn't quite remember what they were designed for.

"Radio ahead to the ER—they'll need to be ready to move when we get there."

"Come on, kid. You're too young to want to find out what's on the other side. Stay with us."

Stay with you? I was never there to start with.

FLORIDA

May 3, 9:50 a.m.

"All right, I've had enough of this shit. Get up."

My door ricochets off the wall in fine Carissa style. Only Anya's the one who threw it open. I stop station-surfing and feign intense fascination with the Weather Channel.

As usual, Anya doesn't take kindly to being ignored. She stalks to the bed and stands directly over me. It's almost like the old days of our early acquaintance. "Hello? Anybody home?"

"Oh, good afternoon." I look up like I've just noticed her there. "Did you come to hear the weather report? By all means, welcome, sit down and enjoy. Looks like Seattle's in for some rain again, would you believe?"

"You're coming to PT today, Dane."

My voice is still saccharine-cheerful and jolly. "The hell I am."

"Let me put it this way. You're going to get up now or I'm going to drag you up. This has gotten ridiculous."

I guess I've been looking for something to pour my anger into because I immediately abandon any pretense of joviality. "I told you I'm not coming! Where the hell do you get off always— always!—thinking you can tell me what I'm going to do and when I'm going to do it?"

Anya rips the remote out of my hand. It takes her two tries. She kills the Weather Channel, then tosses the remote onto the dresser, where it bounces off the varnished brownie-paperweight. She glares down at me.

"I get off thinking that because I actually believe in you and in what you can accomplish." Her voice is low, deadly quiet. "And I'm certainly not going to sit around and watch you undo all the progress you've made in the past two months just because someone else doesn't appreciate what it's worth."

She means my dad.

I don't care. "Can't you comprehend that I don't want the dumbass pep talk?" I've had it. "I'm good and goddamn sick of you people."

"*You* people?" Anya repeats pointedly.

"That's ri—"

"You sweet things okay in here?" Letitia's head pops around the door.

"We're fine!" Anya and I snap at almost the same second, still glaring at one another.

"Okay then, sugars," Letitia says in a placating voice. "Only I never knew the acoustics in this hallway was so good. It's like we got our own private soap-opera show going on out here. Wish you all could hear it." She eyes the two of us like we're misbehaving children, then shakes her head and disappears, pulling the door shut behind her.

Anya and I race to open our mouths. She wins by a micro-second, picks up right where she left off. "*You* people?" she says again.

"That's right. You and everyone else here." Right now I'm not even sure who I'm furious at—Anya, Joel, Letitia—everyone who gets off on deciding what's best for me. As though having a working body gave them the inarguable right. "You all think you have free license to play God with us." I think this is the first time I've ever grouped myself with the rest of the patients here.

"Open your self-centered eyes, Dane. We play God because that's what's asked—no, demanded—of us. Day after day, by all of *you people*." Anya's laugh is short and harsh. "You all want to be fixed, want us to perform miracles we can't guarantee and provide answers we can't give. 'Fix me, cure me, get me exactly back to the way I was. But don't you tell me what I can and can't do!'"

I see she's gearing up for a full-fledged sermon.

"You want to know precisely when you'll be able to walk, run, ski—want us to read your body like it's a freaking equation that has to make perfect sense." She takes a deep breath.

I contemplate the ceiling.

"And we try to give it to you; we let you into our lives and make your recovery our highest priority. We don't leave it behind on our desks when we go home at night—we can't.

"We let ourselves like you, care about you, drive ourselves crazy trying to think of other things we can try, how we can give you your best possible shot. But it's never enough. You'll still turn right around and blame us if it doesn't end up exactly the way you hoped it would. Suddenly it doesn't matter how many hundreds of hours of ourselves we've poured into you.

"And then you have the absolute nerve, you ungrateful brat, to pitch a spoiled little tantrum about me telling you what to do?"

The few remaining threads of my temper unravel and I sit up to continue the fight at least closer to eye to eye with her. "You know, I'd almost started to respect you. But you're nothing different—just another bitch with a goddess complex and high on a power trip.

"You can't handle men, so you have to hide here where they're all too broken to be any threat to your little feminazi ego. No wonder I never did as well in PT as in OT."

A hiss of indrawn breath and the color draining from Anya's face tells me I've scored in a big way.

She doesn't say anything at first. We stare at each other silently for at least thirty seconds.

When she does speak, I can barely hear her.

"Then we're even, because I was wrong about you, too." A muscle near her jaw twitches. "You're not worth a ten-second conversation, let alone floor time in my gym."

She walks to the door slowly, woodenly, then turns back.

"We both may have been wrong, but your dad was right. You're not worth it. Go ahead, lie there and rot. I truly don't care."

May 3, 8:00 p.m.

"Hey, what were all those chairs and crap doing in front of your door? They make it pretty hard to get in here, you know."

Scene #342 of the demented, theater-of-the-absurd performance that's become my life. Enter the annoying braided one. Having barged past my makeshift barricade and into my room, now yelling at me through the bathroom door.

"Not hard enough, apparently," I call back.

She waits a few seconds. "I'm not going away, so you might as well come out."

"Can't a person even take a leak in privacy? Get lost!"

"No way. Better shake it off quick, New York!" The bathroom door flies open.

"Jesus!" I yank the fly on my pajama pants shut barely in time, fumbling with the button until it catches.

"No, just me." Carissa saunters in and perches on the toilet that I've thankfully just vacated, parking her butt on the tank and resting her feet on the closed lid. "But you can think of me as your personal messiah if you really want to—I don't mind."

I spin my chair around to face her. "Whatever you could possibly want this time, I'm not interested. I'm not baking with you.

I'm not offering my bed for your lounging convenience, and I haven't got the energy to listen to you complain about your life." My voice echoes off the green tiled walls as I turn away and pull up to the sink. "I've actually had other things to deal with recently."

Carissa's reflection watches me in the mirror as I wash my hands. "Yeah, I heard what happened with your dad." Her voice is unusually serious. "And I didn't come here just to talk about me."

"If you're here to join the get-Dane-back-to-work brigade, you can save it," I tell her. "I'm done with it—all of it."

Carissa fiddles idly with the toilet handle. "So what're you going to do—hide out here for the rest of your life?"

"Maybe," I say to her reflection. "Why do you care, anyway?"

She looks at me hard. "You're aware that you were an absolute prick to Anya, right?" she says, ignoring my question.

"For God's sake, if you don't like what I have to say, then stop listening in on my conversations!"

"Listening in, my ass." Carissa's fidgeting fingers push the handle. Unfortunately, the ensuing flush doesn't carry her down the pipe along with it. "There were probably deaf people over in Port Charlotte who heard you guys going at it. I can't help it if you don't care who hears you lose your cool, New York, so don't blame me for it."

I can't argue that one, so I don't answer at all. Instead, I head for the door back into my bedroom. Carissa jumps off the toilet and cuts in front of me.

I'm too tired to fight with her. I just sit there wordlessly, waiting for whatever she's clearly itching to say. She stares back at me, leaning against the closed door.

"I'm serious. Why'd you jump all over Anya like that? She was just trying to help, since you're doing such a piss-poor job of helping yourself these days."

My head hurts. I rub my forehead in hard circles. "Were you only policing my behavior, or did you happen to notice she said some shitty things to me, too?"

"I heard."

"Well? She came out and told me I wasn't worth working with anymore." I clench my teeth. "Just like my dad thinks."

Carissa shakes her head. "Come on, she just said that because you were being such a prize asshole."

"Yeah, so much for professionalism. Isn't she supposed to be the adult here?"

"You both are. And no, neither of you were. But I would have yelled at you, too. You hurt her feelings."

I laugh sarcastically. "Impossible. Don't you have to care about something for it to be able to hurt you? We're talking about Ms. Absolute Zero here, remember?"

Carissa crosses her arms. "Doesn't care, huh? Who is it that keeps on going one more pointless round with my dad day after day after day? Who lets my stupid mother blame her over and over for not being able to conjure some miracle to resurrect a living corpse?"

She reaches over and flicks me on the arm. "This is one thing you can trust me on. I've been riding this hospital-go-round a hell of a lot longer than you have. You learn which ones are just putting in floor time for a paycheck and which ones actually give a damn."

Even in the unlikely event that Carissa's right about Anya, it still doesn't matter.

"I'm not doing any more therapy. There's no point."

"Yeah? How'd you figure that one out?"

"In case you haven't noticed, I still can't walk!"

"Yet," Carissa says.

"Maybe never." Anger and fear curdle together inside me as I say the words that were once unthinkable.

The possibility I'd never let myself even consider.

"So you'll waste your time sitting on your ass feeling sorry for yourself instead of finding out?" Her voice is leaking sarcasm all over. "Brilliant plan, New York. Really inspired."

"And what if I do try and find out?" I challenge her. "I'm never going to be the way I was before."

Carissa shrugs. "Big deal."

"Excuse me?"

"You heard me," she says. "Big fucking deal. Do you know how absolutely high on life I'd be if my dad had half—no, 10 percent of the chance you've got?"

I don't have an answer for that.

Carissa kicks at the doorjamb. "So what if you don't know exactly how it's going to wind up? Who the hell says you have to be perfect for people to give a damn about you?"

"Ask my dad."

"I only ask people whose opinions I respect."

I have to laugh a little. "Liar. You've asked mine once or twice."

"Yeah." She doesn't laugh back. I give her a quizzical look.

"I thought you said everyone in this place was useless," I say, gesturing around us.

Carissa rolls her eyes. "Maybe my social isolation's finally sent me over the deep end." She allows herself a small grin. "Oh, I guess it's possible that you're not a complete waste of skin."

"I must have mistaken you for someone else. That sounded almost human," I tell her. "Since your opinion of me is so high, would you mind letting me out of the bathroom now?" Surprisingly, Carissa steps aside and I go back into my room.

She trails after me. "So are you going to get your ass back into rehab and prove your stupid dad wrong?"

"I've already answered that question for you today," I say over my shoulder as I swing myself back into bed.

Carissa narrows her eyes. "I thought the answer might have changed."

"Sorry." I pick up my iPod from the nightstand and start browsing through the menu.

"So I've just been completely wasting my breath on you? Christ, you're even dumber than I thought."

I look up at her for a second. "What, you thought that coming in and rattling off a little inspirational sermon would make me do a one-eighty and fix everything? Sorry, but no thanks. Your theory's crap." I drop my eyes and flip faster through the menu. Why does every damn song seem to have a string of memories of Elise attached?

"Oh, really?"

"It's not just my dad. After I got Guillain-Barré, I obviously wasn't good enough for Elise, either."

Tell me I didn't just say that out loud. And tell me that wasn't my voice shaking a tiny bit as I said it.

I'm not looking at her, but I feel the mattress give as Carissa sits down beside me. Her voice is soft, serious.

"Come on, New York. Even you're not that dumb. From what I gather, Elise wasn't the kind of person who'd leave you because you couldn't do or say something." She tries to meet my eyes; I don't let her.

"I'm guessing she left because of what you chose—or chose not—to do and say when you actually could."

"Leave. Please." My teeth are clenched so tight my jaw aches.

"What?"

"I know you heard me." I pick a random song, stuff in my earbuds, and crank the volume.

Carissa tries a few more times to provoke me, but I pretend I can't hear her over the music. Eventually, she gets frustrated talking to my back. "Everyone hurts, you know," she snaps finally, standing up. "That's why nobody believes you when you try to convince the world you don't." She starts to walk away, then stops.

"Not that you care about my life, but something worthwhile is actually happening for me. Mom's going away for the night, and I'm finally getting the chance to do something to help my dad."

"Help him?" The words come out before I can stop them.

"That's right. So if you want to say good-bye or anything, better get it done before Thursday night."

What? I can't have heard that right. I finally roll over, pulling out my earbuds as I do. But she's gone.

May 4, way before normal working hours

I'm only half-conscious, but I can tell someone's in my room yet again. I fully intend to start demanding a cover charge at the door.

"You awake?" a voice whispers.

"Slightly." I open my eyes as Anya collapses into a chair next to my bed, looking like something just spit her out. There are shadows under her eyes, her face is blotchy, and I'd bet some serious money that she's down a good eight hours of sleep.

Since I was up most of the night myself, doing mental warfare with everything Carissa slapped me with last night I probably look about as good as Anya does.

We aim our eyes anywhere but at each other for a minute. I guess we both said some things we shouldn't have yesterday, and now nobody seems to know how to go about repairing the damage. I finally break the silence.

"You don't look so hot."

Anya laughs shortly. "Makes two of us," she says, rubbing her fists into her puffy eyes.

"Yeah." My own eyes are still barely open.

She looks directly at me then. "Look, Dane, I was way out of line yesterday—"

I interrupt her. "Forget it—it's okay." I'm not exactly proud of myself, either.

She shakes her head. "No, it really isn't. I had absolutely no right to say what I did, and it wasn't true." She leans forward and tosses something onto my bed. "Here. Take a look, okay?"

The something is a large manila envelope. I give Anya a curious glance, then work the flap open. As I lift it free, a stack of pictures slides out and lands facedown on my blanket. I turn the pile over, and my stomach does a somersault.

The first picture is a close-up shot of a young woman's naked torso. But any thrill that could potentially ignite is completely killed by the bruised rainbow of purple, green, and yellow that blossoms across the shoulders and down across breasts and stomach. I look up at Anya. Her face is blank.

"Keep going," she says. So I do.

Taken from every conceivable angle, the pictures show a conglomeration of body parts in various degrees of physical damage. An upper arm marked with the purple imprint of fingers. A raw, shiny patch on a thigh that looks like a burn. The pictures are taken from so close up that they look disjointed, like they don't belong to an actual person.

Until I flip to the last few prints, and a face is staring back at me through the one blue eye that isn't swollen shut. A face I know. A couple freckles are still visible on the scattered unbruised areas, and the long red hair is matted together in places with clumps of something dark and sticky. I swallow down the watery feeling that's trying to rise in my throat and raise my eyes to Anya's.

"I know. It was a bad hair day, wasn't it?" Her voice is deliberately light, her face still chameleon-hidden.

Everybody hurts. Carissa's words echo through my brain. Joel wasn't exaggerating at all. Looks like I was the one who was dead wrong. "When was this?" I ask.

"About a year and a half ago." Anya picks up the picture on top and studies it like she's trying to recognize some fragment of herself in the broken image on the paper. "You know what the funniest thing about it was?"

I haven't a clue what could possibly be funny about this.

She continues, "The worse he was to me, the harder I tried to please him. It was like I had some twisted need to prove to him that I deserved to be treated decently." She laughs. "You see how successful I was," she says, waving a hand at the pictures. "I was so screwed up that I actually thought I was the one with the problem."

"I'm not sure I understand why you're showing me these." It had to have been humiliating to even let some cop or doctor take these pictures in the first place. Why is she voluntarily showing something so personal to me—probably her absolute least favorite patient? Who, if I'm honest with myself, has never even been particularly decent to her from the start?

Anya sighs. "Because I feel like shit about what I said to you yesterday. And I also realized that I'm not the only one who's letting an abusive history adversely affect my life."

"Nobody's ever beaten me up," I say quickly.

"Not on the outside, maybe," Anya counters.

I think of my dad in the therapy room, yelling at me for not being able to walk. My eyes close at the humiliating memory of how that made me try even harder to give him what he wanted. To be what he expected me to be. I don't say anything, but the unexpected touch of Anya's hand on mine makes me open my eyes again.

"You know, Dane, we're a lot more alike than I ever would have guessed when I first met you." She's leaning forward, looking at me with intense eyes.

"You mean we're both stubborn as hell and not particularly user-friendly?" I say, only half-jokingly.

"Yeah, but not just that," she says. "If we're not careful, we're both going to end up letting our pasts screw up our futures." She sighs. "You were right when you said I have a problem with men."

I glance back at the pile of pictures on the bed between us. "I didn't mean—"

"It's okay," she cuts me off. "It's completely true. I haven't had any kind of relationship since all this happened, and I don't know if I'll ever be able to. How can I, when I can barely even bring myself to trust anyone?"

I think of Joel. Even a cynic like me can see what a great person he is and that he'd inflict serious self-harm before he'd ever do anything to hurt Anya.

"You know that Joel's got a thing for you?" Somehow, saying that now doesn't feel like I'm selling Joel out.

Anya smiles a little. "I know. Joel's been a good friend."

"But he doesn't do it for you?"

"It's not that. I just can't afford to let him be more than my friend."

"He's a good guy," I say. I'm starting to sound like Joel's marketing team.

"The best," Anya says. "I'm probably missing out on something wonderful, too. But there's always this nasty little voice camped out in my head, telling me that if I let him in too far, he'll turn mean. Just like Chris did."

"But Joel's not like that."

"No, he isn't." Anya sighs again. "See—I'm my own worst enemy."

Letting our pasts screw up our future. It's clear that Anya's got one hand on the door handle, so to speak, and suddenly I can't help wondering if I did the same thing with Elise. Was I just waiting for her to slip up, to do something to prove that she really didn't care about me?

"Look, enough about me," Anya says, scooping the pictures back into the envelope. "I just wanted to tell you that when you decide to come back to therapy, make sure it's for yourself, okay? You are worth it."

May 4, 10:30 a.m.

The alligator finally caught the anhinga he's been stalking for the past forty-five minutes. Through the binoculars, I look just in time to see the jaws auger shut around the bird. A strangled squawk, a frantic splashing, then nothing but the rippled surface of the pond as it closes over them both.

I'm sort of bummed to see the anhinga go down, and not just because I enjoyed watching it forage.

I came outside right after Anya left my room this morning, and I've been here ever since. After talking to her, and Carissa yesterday, I finally realize that I'm not fooling anyone. Not even myself anymore.

So I have to suck it up and stop lying to myself about Elise. I don't want to think about it, but I know why she really left. I've spent the past two months refusing to acknowledge it, but that doesn't change the truth.

I want it to, but it doesn't.

It was after I got to the hospital, and it could have been two days or two weeks for all I knew. I'd been hooked up to a machine that was breathing for me and nobody was telling me anything. But from the conversations going on over my head, I was starting to get the picture that I probably wouldn't be dying anytime soon. Someone had called my parents, and they were in and out of my room with the hospital people, being told about mysterious things like plasma exchange and immunoglobulin treatment and rehab options. Once in a while, almost as an afterthought, someone would tell me that I was going to be okay.

I tried to believe them, but nothing was feeling okay at that point. My body was still completely dead, my lips were raw from the breathing tube stuffed between them, and I had no idea where Elise was. I remembered she'd been with me when I was moved from the ER to an ICU room, but then I was sort of out of it for a bit. When I woke up, she was gone.

I wasn't ever alone, technically, with everything going on. People were coming and going pretty constantly for a while. But it wasn't until things quieted down that Elise showed up again, and it wasn't until she did that I realized how much I'd been wanting her.

"Dane?" I opened my eyes at the sound of her voice. There were flecks of snow melting in the dark waves of Elise's hair and water beading the surface of her red parka. She traced her cold fingers along the strips of tape that crossed my cheeks to secure the ventilator tube. They slid around to cup the side of my face, and I suddenly wanted desperately to be able to turn my mouth into her hand.

But I couldn't, of course. All I could do was lie there and flick my eyes back and forth like some sort of deranged Morse code.

For a while, Elise didn't say much, which was a welcome change after all the recent commotion. She just sat on the edge of the bed, her hand resting on my chest and moving with the rhythm of the ventilator. I felt the balled-up wad of tension and fear in my stomach slowly start to unwind for the first time in days. I had to keep sliding my eyes way to the left to look at her, but I didn't care. Somehow, at that moment, it seemed like I wanted to keep looking at her forever.

Then Elise started talking. "I'm sorry I didn't come sooner. I know I should have." Her head was dropped, her hair hiding her face. "I had a lot to think about."

I didn't really understand what she meant by that, but I was just glad to have her there now.

Elise lifted her head then and her eyes were shiny, wet-looking. "You're going to be okay, Dane. I talked to one of the nurses, and he explained to me about this Guillain-Barré thing. It's not permanent or anything." She smiled, a little shakily. "Especially not for a perfectionist like you, right?"

Something was wrong. I could tell. Elise was always the epitome of calm control, even in a setting like this. If she knew I was going to be fine, what was it that had her so upset?

Elise leaned forward then, so I could see her face without moving my eyes. She opened her mouth, closed it. Opened it again.

"Dane, I can't stay with you."

Whatever was in my IV had to be messing with me. I couldn't have heard that right.

Elise's eyes overflowed onto her cheeks, but her voice was calm, strong. "I'm sorry, but I just can't be in a relationship with someone who operates on convenience principles. You've treated me as an afterthought for over a year now, and somehow I've been weak or stupid enough to allow that. But it's been taking me apart, Dane. One piece at a time."

What? The words were ricocheting through my mind, but that was as far as I could bring them, thanks to my paralyzed voice muscles.

Her tears were running thick now. "I'm so sorry to do this now, but I have to. I have to do it while you still can't talk. This is the only time you won't be able to take me apart with your words, when you actually have to listen to what I'm saying." She took a big, ragged breath and kept going.

"If I wait, it'll just be like it always was. You'll be able to take whatever I say and turn it back and around until you've convinced yourself—and me, against everything I know to be true—that it was my own perception of things that was screwed up, not you. I love you, Dane, but I have to leave, because loving you is making me not like myself."

A thousand things—arguments, rationalizations, imprecations—were crashing through my brain, but I had absolutely no way to articulate any of them. As much as I wanted to cover my ears and drown her out, I had no choice but to keep on listening, a sick wave of panic blossoming from somewhere deep in my gut.

"You almost had me convinced, too. That a commensalistic relationship could work for us. Each one benefits independently of the other. Maybe it works for crabs and anemones." She shook her head, wiped a hand across her eyes. "But it's not enough for me. Not even close."

She stood up then and reached into the pocket of her parka for something. "I brought this for you," she said, holding up the tiny wooden loon. "It made me think of Tooley Pond. Remember the first time you and I went there? I actually thought you were taking me because you thought I'd enjoy it, not just because you needed somebody to balance out the canoe." She shook her head again, smiling through tears. "Stupid, right?"

She opened my hand, slipped the bird inside, and closed my dead fingers around it. Then she knelt down and kissed me, tears dropping off her cheeks onto mine, and stood up again. "I finally realized that liking to give doesn't mean you have to settle for never having someone reciprocate." She closed her eyes for a second, then gave me that intense, thought-bouncing stare I'd thought I knew so well. Her tick-tock look, I've always called it.

"I deserve more than that, Dane. And someday, I hope you will, too." Elise wiped the rest of the tears from her face and walked out.

Now my stupid face is the one that's wet.

Perception's everything, isn't it? Look at Anya—she can't even have a clear view of someone as great as Joel. And I'm finally admitting to myself that I did the same thing with Elise. Jeff always knew how amazing she is. So did everyone else.

Oh, I'm sure I knew on some level, too. I just never acted like I did. That way, I could pretend it didn't matter.

Joke's on me. She left anyway. And it was my own fault.

I look at the spot where the alligator just took the anhinga down. Then I look down at my wheelchair and think about what it might mean to be stuck with it permanently.

Survival of the fittest, Darwin said. So what the hell are the rest of us supposed to do? The ones who are human, imperfect, each weak or broken or malfunctioning in our own bizarre ways?

I screwed it up.

Elise, I do love you.

Why did that take me so fucking long to figure out?

May 8, 3:34 a.m.

A soft noise startles me awake. After I roll over, it takes a few seconds to figure out what the sound was. It finally hits me that the half circle of light that always shines in from the hallway at night isn't there. The click I heard was the sound of my door being pulled shut. The nurses never close my door, especially at night.

Then I remember that it's Thursday. And in my head I hear Carissa's voice trying to provoke me, telling me her mom was going away, and that she was finally going to do something about her dad.

I pull on a sweatshirt and swing myself into my wheelchair, then peer through the blinds on the inside window. The nurses' desk is empty. I look across the hall.

Robert's door is closed.

Now I know that Carissa wasn't just talking. She meant exactly what she said.

When I open the door, I almost don't recognize Carissa at first because I've never seen her hair not braided. It falls way down her back, loose and silky. She's sitting motionless in a chair beside Robert's bed, staring down at the same frozen, gaping expression that's always on his face. Her head jerks up when I ease the door open, then turns away when she sees it's me.

"Go away." Her voice doesn't have any of the maddening, smart-ass drawl I'm so used to hearing from her. She just sounds tired. Burnt.

"What are you doing?" I say, wheeling the rest of the way into the room and pulling up beside her.

"Saying good-bye." She doesn't look up. "But I'm about done now, so if you'll do me a favor and get lost, I'll get on with things."

"What do you mean, get on with things?"

"I already explained it to you once," Carissa says. "You were too busy playing pity party to pay any attention." She shoves her chair back and stands up. "So don't get all curious on me now, for God's sake." She stops by Robert's dresser for a second, running a finger over the picture of her seven-year-old self, complete with gap teeth and soccer ball and properly functioning daddy. Then she walks over to the ventilator whooshing on its stand beside Robert's bed. She reaches for the alarm button, pauses, and looks back at me.

"Leave, Dane. Now."

She can't be serious. "Why? You really think you're going to kill your dad?"

Carissa doesn't even blink. "Well spotted, New York. So I'd leave now if I were you. You're not a minor, so you could probably get in some trouble if you stick around while I do this."

"And you think you won't?" This is insane. "I don't care if you are a minor—you do this, and you'll be in some serious shit, Carissa." She can't possibly think she'll get away with just offing her dad. Can she?

Carissa throws me a smile devoid of any visible emotion. "At this point, I truly couldn't care less."

"You will when it completely screws up your life."

Her dead smile breaks into a hollow laugh. "You mean the great, nonscrewed-up life I've got now?"

"You know what I mean," I say.

"And this doesn't have anything to do with you, New York," she says, glaring at me. "Would you just go?"

I don't. We stare at each other. Carissa shrugs.

"Your choice," she says. Her hand snakes out to the ventilator alarm and shuts it off.

I turn it back on.

She turns it off.

I turn it on.

"Stop it!" She hits me in the jaw. Hard. I'm not ready for it, and it throws me for a second. But I still manage to grab her wrists and pull her away from the alarm before she can turn it off again. We struggle for a minute. My leverage isn't the best since I'm sitting and she's standing. And Carissa's fighting dirty, kicking me in the shins, stomping on my feet, even hauling off and slamming her knee into my chest once or twice. But even off my feet, I'm still strong enough to hold her off and away from the alarm.

Not quite as useless as you thought, Dad.

I twist down on her arms, not to hurt her, just to force her closer to my level. She finally drops to her knees, still fighting me.

"Carissa. You can't do this."

"Let me go!"

"Listen to me. Killing your dad isn't going to fix your life. It's going to wreck it."

"I don't care!" She bites my forearm, almost making me lose my grip. But I hold onto her. And suddenly she stops fighting and just stares at me. She's crying, crying hard and without even thinking about it, I let go of her wrists and pull her against me. She hits me a few more times, stops, and goes limp, still swearing at me through the tears.

"Please, Dane." The words are barely whispered. "Let me do it. It's not just for me, I swear it isn't." Carissa raises her teary face for a second. "Look at him. It's not right. He deserves some dignity."

I look over her head to Robert's Halloween grimace and twisted-up arms and legs. An image of Angelica at Jeff's party flashes through my memory—passed out, wasted—and everybody enjoying the show instead of stepping in to help.

No, it isn't right. Nothing about this whole twisted situation is right. But even as much as I might agree with Carissa on this, I still can't let her do it—to herself or to her dad. Robert's about as ill-adapted for survival as any organism I've ever known, but sitting by and doing nothing now would be saying he doesn't deserve that stupid, tiny fraction of a chance, no matter how infinitesimal.

I may not believe in that chance—and I'm pretty sure I don't—but I can't be the one to let it be actively taken away. I don't have the right.

We both jump at the sound of junk gurgling in Robert's airway. The ventilator alarm shrills into the quiet, dark hospital air, not quite as loudly as usual. I must not have put the volume completely back up when I turned the alarm back on. I glance over my shoulder through the window to the nurses' station. Still empty. No respiratory therapist, either.

Minutes pass. Carissa turns in my arms to look at Robert. He's clearly having some more trouble now, the gurgling getting more wet and sticky. "I'm going to do it," she whispers, making a move to pull away from me and turn the alarm back off. But she barely fights against me this time. I realize that, on some level, she wants me to stop her.

So I just hold her, letting her bury her face in my sweatshirt and pound her fists against my chest. She's shaking. So am I, a little. The rattle coming from Robert's bed is louder, thicker. The alarm's still going off. What happens now is no longer up to us.

There's a pounding of sneakered feet behind us, and the third-shift nurse comes running in, stale cigarette smell clinging to her scrubs. "Why didn't you tell me his alarm was going off?" she blusters, like she wasn't just on a twenty-minute smoke break instead of watching her patients. She pushes her way between us and Robert and starts suctioning him.

"Come on, Robert. Cough it on up." Blood-tinged gunk sucks out through the tube into the plastic collecting thing. "There we go." Robert's eyes dart spastically, like he's searching for something. His lips twitch as uselessly as a landed fish dying on a river-bank. I look at a picture over the dresser, the one of Robert and the other firefighters geared up beside the pumper truck.

The nurse glances over her shoulder at us as she finishes. "Honey, I know he's cute," she tells Carissa, gesturing at me, "but you really should pay more attention." She chuckles. "Why, just imagine what could have happened to your daddy if I hadn't been here!"

Carissa doesn't even look up.

The alarms get reset.

The nurse leaves, and it's only the three of us again.

"I hate you," Carissa whispers. Her voice is muffled against my chest, her hands curled around damp fistfuls of my sweatshirt. "I really do."

"I know." I slide my hand over her hair, smoothing it. I never did this with Elise. I wish I had. "I know."

But at least someone finally hates me because I did the right thing.

May 17, 10:25 a.m.

"So word's out that you've decided to stay with us a bit longer," Anya says as she fiddles with the screws that adjust the parallel bars.

Yes, I finally got my ass back into rehab.

"Is that what they're spreading around now?" I say, raising my eyebrows and pretending to be amazed.

It's true. Much to my surprise, my parents actually came back to see me after a week. Much to my shock, my father seemed just the slightest bit apologetic about how he acted. He didn't say as much, of course, but he did tell me I could come back north and finish rehab someplace closer to home if I wanted.

I told him I was staying here. Now that I've finally realized I can't do this all on my own, I don't want to leave the only real support system I have at the moment. At least not until I've found out just how much better I'm going to get. Dad was less than thrilled when he found out about my plan to hold off on summer school and college in the fall. For now, anyway. But it's my life, and I don't see any reason to rush things before I'm ready for them.

So it looks like I'll be staying here at the veggie ranch, at least for another month or so. That means putting up with Letitia's stupid pet names, early morning wildlife hunts with Isaac, butting heads with Anya, and trying to coerce Joel into letting us do OT outside. There are worse things.

There are two people, though, who won't be here.

"It's quiet around here since Carissa's been gone, huh?" I say.

"Very." Anya finishes changing the height of the bars, then swings herself up to sit sideways across them. "Are you going to keep in touch with her?"

"Not sure. Maybe." Robert's not a patient here anymore. Eva came back from visiting a rehab hospital farther west last week and announced that she was taking Robert there.

So they've all gone. Eva, I guess, to chase another pipe dream of a miracle cure for her husband, and Carissa once again dragged along for the ride. As for Robert, I doubt it matters to him at all.

Carissa didn't say much before she left. She did come and tell me good-bye, but it was obvious she was still angry with me. Maybe. I guess it's hard to face someone after they've seen you break.

I'll miss her, though. So I'll probably give it a little time, then look her up. I'm curious to see what she'll do with her life once she actually has some control over it.

I also wonder how long it'll be until she finds another careless night-shift nurse who takes long smoke breaks.

"Hey, are you guys talking or working in here?" We both turn to see Joel lounging in the doorway.

"Mind your own business, Costello, or I'll hide your inhaler." Anya jumps off the parallel bars and tosses one of the big exercise balls at him.

He dodges it and disappears down the hallway, laughing.

"Then you can rescue me again!" his voice trails back to us.

"Pain in the ass," Anya grumbles good-naturedly, shaking her head.

I park my chair in the parallel bars and set the brakes. "So when are you going on a date with him?"

"You mind your own business, too," she says. But she's smiling a little. "I don't know. Sometime. Maybe."

"Well, get moving," I tell her. "Nobody wants to wait around forever." I touch the wooden loon in my pocket and think about what I'm going to say to Elise when I finally get up the nerve. I think about it whenever I look at the picture she sent from that long-ago day at Walden and remember how beautiful she looked asleep in the moonlight. I don't have a clue what she's thinking, or if she's with Jeff or anyone else now, or if she'll even talk to me at all. It's probably way too late to try and fix things with her anyway. But I have to try. I owe it to both of us.

Anya rolls her eyes at my last comment as she pulls her stool into the parallel bars to sit in front of me.

"Anya?"

"What?"

"What if I don't get it all back?"

"Sorry. Just dropped my crystal ball off at the cleaner's."

"I'm serious."

She sits back and looks at me. "You want my honest opinion?"

I nod.

"I think you've already gotten more back than you had before."

"Very inspirational," I tell her. "Now answer me for real."

"For real?" Anya smiles. "I guess we'll find out when we get there, won't we? Now get up."

I grab the bars with both hands, she pulls me forward by my hips, and I'm standing. Not quite by myself.

Not yet.